I0772743

PETER LOUCKS

Graham Crackery: Food Detective

The Case of The Misplaced Peppercorn Pipe

First edition

ISBN: 979-8-218-09326-6

Editing by Salima Alikhan
Illustration by Sunny Duran
Editing by Adrienne Kisner

This book was professionally typeset on Reedsy.
Find out more at reedsy.com

For Oliver

Contents

GRAHAM
CRACKERY
FOOD DETECTIVE

1

Prologue

Fresh off another case, Graham Crackery: Food Detective was baked into a corner. With only a pretzel-rod pool cue in his hand, Graham was staring down a bunch of sticky, scummy bears — members of The Gummy Family.

He'd been following them all day, watching from the shadows as they annoyed, fought, and terrorized each and every Food they came across in Kitchentown. Graham wasn't interfering just yet; he didn't need CHEESE officers after him again. The detective was both in and outside the law – neither of which stopped him from taking it into his own hands.

After several incidents throughout the day, Graham was tired of watching the Gummy gang commit crimes, hurt others in Kitchentown, and face no accountability. The CHEESE always arrived too late, long after the Gummy gang departed. Now, finally, as he was accustomed to, Graham took matters into his own hands and followed the gang into a pool hall.

Detective Crackery's two biggest problems were keeping his patience and his mouth in check; he had a knack for saying about five words more than he should, about two minutes after he shouldn't.

"Listen pal, we're done with your cherry pit. You gonna tell us why you're tailing us all day, or we can take you apart, piece-by-piece. Crumblin' you in two," growled Yellow Gummy Jr; son of the inscrutable and rarely seen Yellow Gummy Sr., head of the Gummy family.

"*Crumblin'* in two? Really? You got me quaking in my..." Graham smirked just as Yellow Gummy Jr. landed a fast blow right to the detective's breadbasket.

Graham doubled over, trying to catch his breath. He knew when he walked into Peppy's Pool Hall to bust the Gummy gang for their crimes, it could end up like this. But, like his Graham-mom taught him, 'Don't shy away from a bumbling bully. Put them back in their place and they won't bother you again.'

The words filled the detective with a strong and blustery second wind. With a big swing came a bigger miss, right passed Yellow Jr's hulking, yet nimble frame.

"Oh fud..."

Before Graham could finish saying the word, the back of his head cracked, and his world went dark.

Chapter One: The Case of the Misplaced Peppercorn Pipe

Present Day
The Fridge was especially cool this time of year. Graham and Marsha enjoyed their favorite room at the Crisper Inn...
Graham's eye shot open while pain coursed through his body. His other eye would have opened if it wasn't for the bone-crunching the defeated detective had taken again last night.

Wiping the crumbs from his crusty eyes, Graham realized he couldn't remember how he had gotten home... only the dreamy visions of the past fading from his swimming head.

The disgruntled detective grunted as he squared over in bed to finally get up and see the time – 2:00 pm. Too late to let anyone know he had just woken up and too early to stay in and call the day the mistake that it was.

His dream of Marsha in the cool, perfect air was fading faster than his memory of what happened last night. After the pretzel-pool cue dropped from his hand, his slim, weathered, and 6-inch tall frame, dropped even harder to the pool hall floor.

Only a sticky son of a biscuit would hit him from behind.

The Gummy's had been increasingly problematic for Graham the last few months, but if you asked them, they'd say it was Graham who was the persistent pest. The reality was they were constantly boiling each other up. Graham's efforts to clean up Kitchentown were always thwarted by the greedy, gooey bears – constantly mucking up the system for their own gain. The Gummy's had one goal – own Kitchentown – one way or another.

"I'll show him 'crumblin' next time." Graham huffed and stumbled into the bathroom. His imbalance, much like his mood, was off, causing him to fall, once again, to the floor.

"Get it together, Crackery." he mumbled, slowly picking himself off the floor. Crumbs scattered everywhere from his body. He was beginning to crack up again. He couldn't go full crack up anymore, not after last time.

Being a detective in this town wasn't easy for Graham, thanks solely to the Gummy Family. Graham was once a fresh-faced detective ready and willing to take on the world. Yet, as it happened all too often, any Food that tried to clean up this city was met with the full force of the Gummy's. Those willing to stand up against Gummy rule quickly became hard-boiled and would either give up or get in on the take. Graham always tried to dissuade any aspiring detective, who looked up to him, from this path.

One young sprout in particular, Artie Chokerode, would drive around Kitchentown looking for Graham to help him with his work. The detective had the unsavory duty to ignore the little stalker so as not to get her in any unnecessary trouble.

Throughout the course of Graham's career as a Food Detective, he'd seen his fair share of how Kitchentown could be exceedingly fresh and devastatingly sour – especially the recent loss of Marsha. It hadn't been more than a month since Marsha's disappearance, since Graham's last crack up, since the last time things made sense.

Graham shuffled over to his front door and opened it to the blistering sun that came in through the big window. Squinting as the first reminder of vitamin D assaulted his eyes, he grabbed this morning's long-forgotten paper and rapidly drew back indoors to the refreshing darkness. Graham hadn't always been this much of a hermit. But, these days, nothing else out in the town mattered to Graham. Not his reputation, not his hygiene, and not the fact that all of his cases had gone cold.

The derelict detective unfolded the paper to a startling headline from the Kitchentown Crier:

"*Kitchentown in Chaos.*"

Graham folded and unfolded the paper while simultaneously blinking as if to wake himself (or maybe just his eyes) up; that headline didn't seem right. The byline revealed the writer to be none other than city-renowned Mabel Seerup, making the shocking headline scarier than normal. Mabel was never one to dress up a story for readership. 'The truth was always more interesting,' she often said.

Graham put the paper down to get a pair of specs to see better. Shuffling through what could only be described as a dank den of obsession, Graham walked down the hallway. The walls were coated with printed-out pictures of Gummy Family activity throughout the last several months. A red, vein-like network of Twizzle-string all led to Yellow Gummy Sr with Yellow Gummy Jr as his number two bear. Graham was still a ways off from catching the corrupt crime family.

Kitchentown hadn't always been a booming city; there were times of squalor and emptiness. Back in those days, good Food went bad and turned to less-than-savory ways to make a buck.

The Gummy Family was always there: rotund and sticky arms wide open. They were thought of as a safety net in some ways for lower fortunate Food. Kitchentown didn't feel that Mayor Naise was doing anything of any value, so many Foods joined in with the Gummy way.

This helped spread the Gummy's filth to other parts of Kitchentown and incentivized the youth of the city to forgo hard work and let Kitchentown go to rot. It became a hot dog eat hot dog world.

Like a wave, every few months or so, a string of Food would expire. Months later, they'd pop up looking similar, yet somehow completely different. You didn't know who in the town was legit and who wasn't at this point.

These ex-expired Food, or Leftovers, as they were non-affectionately called, would relocate to new parts of Kitchentown with fresh identities and open a small business of some random sort to assist in laundering the Gummy's dirty money. The CHEESE none the wiser and the town none the richer.

It was also a not-so-well-kept secret that the Gummy's employed some rotten Food, a mold, on the inside of the CHEESE station prison, The Jammer.

The "mold" would bake the Gummy's business on the back

end. Sneakily, without the other CHEESE officers knowing, the mold would take a newly incarcerated Food on some random, low-shelf offense.

A temporary expiration date would be assigned to them to fake their passing. Then, the Gummy Family would put the bad Food back onto the streets to run their own business, a laundry service for the Gummy slushie funds. Expiration dates on Food in the city started becoming a commodity. Anyone could purchase a new way out of a bad life and get an undeserved fresh start.

They would just end up in the Gummy's pocket.

Graham rummaged through his room, wading through piles of papers, in order to find his specs. Graham no longer had belongings, he 86'd them right after he lost Marsha. Instead, he collected clues – some from cases past, some other cases as a trophy. A reminder of the ghost of who Graham was.

The last unsolved mystery before his break and breakdown was figuring out more of Marsha's possible demise. The Gummy's had to be involved somehow, he thought. After fumbling through more clues, and finally finding his glasses, Graham walked back along a line connecting Yellow Gummy and his less-than-ideal son, to a string of crimes that had occurred in the town lately.

Graham sat back down and continued reading his paper.

"Over the last several weeks, a series of thefts have rocked the city. Increasing in value and complexity, each crime took more morale, and heart, from its citizens. A Spokes Food for the CHEESE of police, Lieutenant Gouda has been leading the investigation."

Graham rolled his eyes at the mention of the name. Gouda's relationship with Graham, on a good day, was sour. Graham placed partial blame for Marsha's absence on Gouda. Shuddering at his crack-up in the CHEESE station and the way he reacted, Graham remembered taking a big chunk out of Gouda, emotionally and physically.

"The CHEESE has been vigorously investigating each incident but we're warning all local businesses and government buildings to beef up their security. We aren't divulging any leads at the moment however, we do anticipate another spate of these robberies."

Graham swallowed hard. He knew it was time to dust off his hat and get back out there – he was being summoned through the press.

"While some speculate Black Berret, the rarely-seen, Fridge-famous burglar as the culprit, others suspect Gummy involvement."

That was all Graham needed to read.

Gummy involvement.

Graham needed to freshen himself up badly, he could still feel the crumbs chafing down the back of his neck. He knew the best cure for those long nights and getting into trouble with the Gummy's, was his frosting shower. The sweet and healing hot suds kept Graham in the shower for over an hour. Graham's ritual was to essentially meditate, it was the only time he allowed himself to be free of everything but his own self. No thoughts, no worries – just standing there replenishing, putting the crumbs back together – healing for the start of another day.

Wiping away the condensation in the mirror Graham took a long, hard look at himself. His eyelids were still swollen and rearranged. He wore a map of Kitchentown in the cracks on his face and body. Each one represented a new scar, an awful memory mainly of loss.

"Bruised and beaten, but still crackin','' Graham half-smiled as he whispered to himself. It became a mantra for him, he relished the pun. It gave him time to catch up on his health but used all the strength he could muster.

Whistling through his cracked chicklets, Graham sorted through his laundry to find a suitable outfit. Graham was buttoning up the final gumdrop button as his doorbell rang exactly at 5pm, exactly like every single day for the last month. The ringing bell was almost pavlovian for Graham; it meant two things: Cocoa and candied canes.

Graham rushed to get his own hat before swinging open the door to Cocoa's hat already soaring midair towards Graham's head. Graham tried to react with the same speed and accuracy, but those frosting showers can't whip miracles.

Coakley "Cocoa" Lattely Caine, swooped to grab Graham's hat before it fell to the floor next to his expensive ChickenStock Leather Oxfords. Cocoa's cream-colored trilby hat sailed across the room and landed perfectly upon Graham's head. Cocoa was gifted with style and blessed to be missing the curse of the clumsy.

"We've been playing this game for years." Cocoa chuckled, "One day you're going to have to try a little bit to beat me," Cocoa lightly teased Graham, unsure of which Crackery he'd be meeting with today. Like all those grieving, there are good days and bad. Thankfully, and with Cocoa's help, Graham was moving through grief and back into his work at a much quicker pace.

Graham tossed his own jokes back with a shrug, letting Cocoa know who he was dealing with today, "Win, lose, or draw, we're each going to enjoy some of your candy canes, so..." he tailed off in eager anticipation.

On bad days, Cocoa would just give Graham a handful of canes and sit quietly with him. Cocoa took advantage of the good days and was more direct in how he could help his downtrodden detective friend.

"I'm assuming you saw the Crier today." Cocoa jumped right in – he already knew the answer to the question, he just needed to check Graham's reaction.

"Yea, Mabel's piece? I saw it, and I do think it's time for me to get crackin.' I've been out of the game too long and I'm starting to get the itch again, it's just a lot to chew on." Graham felt more spry, like when he first became a detective.

Back in those days, Graham didn't have the luxury of word-of-mouth client gathering, he couldn't even afford a Ham Radio to listen in on the CHEESE Police chatter: he had to walk the beat and find his own cases. He had the energy back then, and he felt it coming back in a way he hadn't in a while, even before Marsha's disappearance.

"Besides," Graham tossed Cocoa's hat back and reached for his own, "The Gummy Family has been rearranging my face and my life for too long. I'm heading into the office, you coming?"

Cocoa, who occasionally freelanced with Graham on less dangerous cases, gathered his things and handed Graham several packets of candied canes.

"I have a few errands to run; this Cane Shop isn't going to build itself. And hey, I appreciate the help in the meantime." Cocoa had a habit of bringing a serious note to the end of their time together.

Graham scoffed, not in offense, but surprise. "There's never a need of thanks or of apologies between us. You're helping me more anyway, that I can assure you."

Graham took his first lick of another cane as he left his apartment, said goodbye to Cocoa, and locked the breadbolt door.

As Graham left, he noticed a taxi idling across from his

apartment waiting to see if Graham would utilize its services. The detective glanced over to see young Artie Chokerode sitting behind the wheel waving. Detective Crackery gave a slight wave back and continued on down the street alone. Artie got the hint, as she had most days, and the car sped off in the other direction. Another day, another young member of Kitchentown being ignored for her own protection. Graham was continuously wary of younger Food brought into the detective game too early.

It was summer in Kitchentown and this time of year was so hot even the massive town window was open.

"Is it pie baking season already?" thought Graham to himself as he rolled up his sleeves, dabbed his forehead with a handkerchief, and took another lick of the cooling cane.

"Hiyah, Detective! How are you? I hope you're havin' a great day!" Graham's neighbor, Penny Pickle, yelled out.

"How's that little gherkin of yours?" Graham asked, waving back. He kept his pace down the street not wanting to slow down and chat. Graham was grateful for the appreciation. He'd stopped a "recruitment" attempt by the Gummy Gang of Penny's son, Petey a few months ago. Graham decided he'd rather not refresh those memories.

"Thanks to you, he's doing great! Keep up the good work!" Penny's voice faded in the distance.

Graham laughed to himself, '*Good* work, *hah!*'

Unlocking the door to his office at the corner of Baking St and Oven Way, Graham wiped away the built-up sweat. Continuously and oppressively hot, Detective Graham Crackery's 'Case Crackers', located at 35 Oven Way, looked bad, smelled bad, and, if you weren't careful walking over the staircase – one wrong step meant a foolish fall into a fiery send-off.

Graham opened his door to the mess he left days ago: old case files, several candy canes all licked-to-the-nub, Insta coco-coffee packets, pictures of friends from a happier time, and, of course, Marsha's picture. Most of those were upside down, too painful for the detective to look at anymore.

Graham put his feet up on the pile of looming memories and to-dos and got right into his voice messages.

"First Message," bleeped the mechanical voice.

"Detective Crackery, this is Randal Radish, my cat is stuck in Broccoli Rob's Park again…" Graham skipped ahead knowing Randal was a little more dramatic than necessary.

"Next Message," chirped the machine once again.

"Mr. Crackery this is your Cookie Card calling, you're 38 days past due on your…." Graham again quickly skipped ahead.

"Next Message:"

Graham's ears perked up when he heard a faint tune being hummed. It was their song, Old Cookie Moon. Her angelic voice hummed as if she was waiting on the other line.

Jumping at the hesitancy of hearing Marsha's voice again, Graham leaped up too fast and knocked over a pile of papers sitting precariously on his desk hitting the forward button on the machine.

"Next Message," said the mechanical voice, this time with what felt to Graham like a flair of defiance.

"No! Go back!" shouted Graham at the machine as he mashed the buttons all at once in a panic until finally hitting the right button.

"Previous Message," it said in agreement.

"Graham, it's Mike Mustardereli, I need you down here right away…" the voice cut out again.

"No more messages."

"I'm cracking up again," Graham whispered to himself.

3

Chapter Two: The Letter

Graham would not go down that route again – hearing or seeing things that weren't there, hoping for things that were hopeless – he couldn't crack up again.

The downtrodden detective rubbed his eyes and went back to throwing away the bills that were piling up higher than the GumDrop State Building; he had business he needed to attend to and feeling sorry for himself wasn't on the honeydew list.

He wound up and threw his last piece of mail at the trash can. However, as it escaped his hand, he noticed something. The smell that accompanied the envelope kicked his memory into overdrive.

Barney's BB-Q Lounge.

In their younger days, Graham, his brother Sylvester, and Cocoa would all shoot a few rounds of Pretzel Stick at Potate's Pool Hall a few times a week. Back then it was still Potate's before selling to Peppy Pepperson.

Sylvester Moore was often mistaken for Graham's twin cracker; much to Sylvester's annoyance. No one remembered Sylvester, it was always Graham who was the more charming of the two. Sylvester spent his whole life hearing the inevitable, 'Graham, is that you?'

Followed by the hollow and disappointed, 'Oh, never mind, I thought you were someone else.' That excitement fading from each pair of eyes pushed Sylvester further and further from compassion to his friends and fellow Food in Kitchentown.

The two diverging Crackers met after each being separately dropped off at the Asparagus J. Veggitray Orphanage. Graham and Sylvester became inseparable after being unable to understand or cope in their new environment. As far as they knew, they were brothers, born from the same Mother, cruel and unforgiving as she was and would be.

Each outing with the three friends ended with the same arrange-

ment: the loser would buy dinner at Barney's, a deal that was more for the fun of it than the challenge. Barney Bracoly, the Lounge's gregarious owner, always fed them on the house. These were the perks of being a friendly Food and striking up conversation at the right time; a gift Graham and Cocoa possessed and one Sylvester never received.

Graham was chowing down as usual on his favorite dish, the Rib-It when he looked across the room. Behind Sylvester, Graham noticed the most beautiful face he'd ever seen. Graham was certainly a lot braver in those days, though some would say immature. He didn't hesitate to not miss this opportunity,

"'Scuse me, miss, would you happen to have any more napkins? I seem to be out." Graham called out to the young Marsha with sauce all over his face and upheld hands. Her only company at the table was a pile of books, a pen in her hair, a few well-worn notebooks, and a steaming cup of coco-coffee.

Without looking up from her book, she handed a napkin forward, presuming it went where it was needed. Graham took it, unphased by the lack of reaction, and decided to hand it back with a sloppy smile, "Not this one, do you have anything a little less, well, used?" he mused to a disinterested Marsha.

Annoyed, she finally looked up, ready to exit the situation, when she noticed the mess all around Graham's mouth. She couldn't help but smirk.

Marsha smiled and took the dirty napkin only to give him an even dirtier one from her empty plate. That was all it took for Marsha to melt Graham's young heart.

Graham left Cocoa with Sylvester to learn as much as he could about this mellow Mallow.

Marsha learned Graham was a fledgling detective. Graham deduced from her books she was studying at the prestigious Murphy's

Law School. Marsha explained she was interning at the Hellman Building in the Fridge. It was clear to both of them Marsha was on to bigger things; she had a real conviction for change in Kitchentown in her eyes. And now Graham was sliding into her view as well.

There was no return address on the invading, yet intoxicating smell of the envelope. It was enough to have Graham tear the mystery letter open without any reservation. Inside he found a mini-magnet message spelling out a horrifying warning:

Detective Crack-Up,

One of your voice messages is not like the other, which one doesn't belong? Here's a clue: A precious piece from a particular place has been pilfered. Find it or you'll see more expirations around the city. Come alone to the Fridge Floor at 8:00pm, this Friday. Hold the CHEESE or you'll be in a huge pickle.

No signature, no return address. Just the nostalgic scent of a long time ago.

One thing he did know was when to involve CHEESE and when to leave them out.

Detective Crackery had a healthy respect for the law enforcement in Kitchentown. There were some on the CHEESE Force he could count on while the other half were just plain stinky.

They claimed to be the collectors of garbage in the city, but they tended to create more.

Graham operated slightly outside of CHEESE's jurisdiction, making his relationship with the arm of the law porous and somewhat mild.

It was getting late and Graham was so distraught he missed the trash cans being noisily knocked over outside. He missed Cocoa's joke apology on the way in. The only thing that wasn't missed was Cocoa's hat toss landing perfectly on his sullen friend's downturned head.

Cocoa rushed over, picked Graham up off the floor, shoved a few canes in his hand, and sat him back down softly at his desk. Graham explosively and quickly filled Cocoa in on the message and now the detective needed time to marinate.

"It's just eating me up right now, is Marsha actually still alive? And now I don't have a choice, but to find what's about to be stolen. I don't know if I have it in me, man..."

Graham slumped further into his chair. Before Coco could provide any respite to his weary friend, Graham put his head in his hands and whispered softly to himself, "What's going on?"

"You know what though?" offered Cocoa positively, "They never did find Marsha when she fell down the Dehydrator chasing after you that night. Plus, you *know* she was a tough cookie and *always* knew what she was doing. Something just doesn't seem right about any of it. "

Graham perked up somewhat at this revelation, "They didn't find her, you're right! She could have melted away, but there would be at least SOME clues about her somewhere?"

"The report must have been fudged," Graham pounded his fist on the table; Cocoa hardly flinched. He'd seen much worse from Graham's crack-ups. Thankfully they were getting less intense and destructive as time moved on.

The Dehydrator was built by the Sink Hotel and sold as a 'paradise of relaxation.' When completed, it would wow the crowd with several spa facilities inside the large infrastructure.

This new outburst of jobs would be another push for The Fridge to be one of the wealthiest Townchips in all of Kitchen-town.

The rest of The Dehydrator was to be used for laundry mats and smoke lounges.

It could also be used by the Gummy family to dispose of any

problems. Problems could be thrown in the back-heater section that powered the entire grid and never seen again.

With the proper understanding of the owner's manual, one could turn up the heat, making a bastion for relaxation. But a melting pot of doom for those unfortunate enough to be thrown in. Putting it next to the Sink Hotel with its signature waterfall wasn't exactly the brightest of designs.

Graham's head began spinning, half from the number of candy canes he'd demolished, half from the number of questions floating around his head like sugar plum fairies:

Are the Gummy's behind this? Is Marsha alive? Is she okay? Should I open one more candy cane?

Cocoa placed a reassuring hand on Graham's shoulder, "You know I'm here for you, always, we're in this until the bitter end." Then with a smile, "Or until I open up my Candy Cane store."

Graham hesitated a moment and took a deep breath. "I know how much you want to help, and you know how much I appreciate it. But, Cocoa, I need to do this alone. Last time..." Graham stopped short. "You just can't come! People get hurt and I...I can't go through this again."

Graham took a deep breath, there would be no crack-ups today. He still needed to let Cocoa know it was okay to leave him, Graham needed time to think anyway.

"It's late and I'm doing alright now, thanks to you. Why don't you head on home, I'm going to get myself organized and figure out my next steps."

Cocoa looked at Graham then scanned the cane wrappers on the ground and the overall unkemptness of the office. He didn't want to leave, but he knew Graham had a process; if he said go, it was time to leave.

4

Chapter Three: Mike's Rare Monuments and Other Strings

Graham woke up early the next morning to take proper care of himself for what lay ahead. Another frosting shower to heal his still broken cracks, a freshly ironed shirt, crisp pants, and, the cherry on top, his signature hat.

Detective Graham Crackery was back!

Graham's habit of needing the Tea-V on 24/7, with an ever-flowing cup of coco-coffee, came in handy for some Break-fasting News, allowing him to get a jump on a case.

"That's why my Doctor prescribed me Eatitall, the only pill to not make you ill."

The commercial faded out as Graham walked back to sit down with his steaming mug to see what was happening this morning in Kitchentown, any leads he could chase before heading down to Mike's place.

Holding his smoldering hot coco-coffee, he sat leaning back and relaxed, but only for the moment.

"And now, KitchenTown News Network brings you all the news you can muster. Featuring Peaches Petunia and Andrew

Appel on the desk, Frankie Dogs with sports, and Kale Williams with the weather. Your KTNN starts rrrrright now!"

Graham's eyes rolled.

"We're back with some Break-Fasting News, exclusively at KTNN. I'm Andrew Appel," Andrew declared.

"And I'm Peaches Petunia. This morning, Yellow Gummy Jr, heir to the Gummy Family fortune, has been forked several times; he is pronounced expired as of early this morning.

Sources indicate he was sleeping in his massive 45-bedroom aluminum-grade, foil mansion when an unknown assailant snuck up and offed Gummy Jr."

Graham's coco-coffee took the unusual journey from mug, to mouth, to Tea-V screen. He wiped his mouth from the remaining drink that had been spat and turned the volume up.

"I guess you could say, he's done," Andrew Appel stared into the camera with a massive grin on his face. **"Get it...stick a fork in me, I'm..."**

Receiving no reaction from his co-anchor or anyone else watching, Andrew continued to awkward silence, **"We're, uh, now going live at CHEESE Headquarters to the CHEESE of Police, Captain Roquefort Bleu. Captain, Good Morning."**

"Good Morning, thanks for baking me into your schedule," grunted Ol' Bleu.

One third of Bleu's career was spent in front of the camera. He was a big fan and loved it, or used to. The limelight and the prestige, at one point, made him seem like the man with the plan boosting his rise to The Captain of CHEESE of Police. Bleu was a talented and creative problem solver, but he had a gruff side. After years of Kitchentown crime rates spiking when the Gummy's came into play, it took its toll on Bleu's house.

He would snap at his staff, quietly, but often loudly, disrespect the head politicians who oversaw CHEESE, and was generally rough around his edges. The rest of the squad nicknamed him Captain Crunch because of the way Bleu would crumble the officers to pieces and spit them out.

Today, he was ready for the cameras hopefully for the last time; his retirement couldn't come soon enough.

Petunia leaned forward as if Bleu was in the room, **"Captain, could you tell us if there are any suspects at this time and who they are?"**

Bleu responded in a way he had many times before, his delivery almost robotic and forced, **"At this time, we aren't able to disclose any of that information. We can say we will be investigating this swiftly. The Gummy family is devastated and asks that you respect their privacy during this difficult time.**

Furthermore, we will be placing all pending criminal investigations against the Gummy's on hold indefinitely until this case is solved and the culprits have been taken into custody."

"Captain, thank you for your time, good luck with this case and we'll check back in with any updates," chirped Peaches.

Bleu immediately took off the earpiece before the anchors could even say goodbye and walked away. He dropped it as he left, leaving the news crew scrambling to pick it up.

Graham was too stunned to speak, but the Tea-V would fill the silence for him.

"Coming up next, we'll be checking in on the annual Peep migration and how it'll affect your weekend. And Black Beret has struck again, find out whose day is going sour next," said Peaches. **"Stick around."**

Graham stood up, allowing the shock to absorb for a few moments.

The commercials came back on to interrupt his thoughts, **"Come down to the Sink Resort, your troubles will flow down the drain as you…"**

Graham shut the Tea–V off.

"Good riddance, ya Yellow Son of a biscuit." Spitting on the floor, the detective turned to walk away, took a lick of his candy cane, and put his bread shoes on to walk out the door and into another day in Kitchentown.

Detective Crackery allowed Artie to drive him to his destination today. He didn't want to walk, nor did he want public transportation; Graham just needed a quiet ride. As he locked his door and walked towards the taxi, Artie, more excited than ever, decided she'd be quiet today and simply drive Graham to his destination.

Artie wanted desperately to help Graham the way her own family had been helped, but patience needed to be part of her strategy. They rode in silence and Graham tossed more than the cab fare with plenty of tip to Artie with a dry, "Thanks, kid."

Graham stepped out of the taxi after having arrived at Mike Mustardereli's Rare Monuments and Other Strings, exit 5 off the Licorice Highway, the last exit before the Fridge. In fact he was so close to it, he could smell the freshness of the Farm and Hammer Homestead on the Fridge's second floor, not far from the capitol, The Hellman Building.

Graham rapped on the door, which began to swing open as he spoke, "Hey Mike, It's Detective Crackery, sorry I'm getting here a day late, I just…"

Graham stopped talking at the sight of Mike Mustardereli stumbling up to the door, out of breath, out of his mind, and less jaundiced than normal.

"Detective, thank you for coming so quickly. Please, this

way." Sweating more than usual and even more out of breath, he waddled back into his store; something was off.

Mike had always been unusually sweaty. When they first met, Graham noticed two things about this yellow ball of anxiety — his uniquely moist handshake and his incredibly quick, if not disassociated, wit. Sadly, the wit part was mostly soggy by the panic and out-of-breath running.

"Mike, first off, calm down, you're as transparent as The Kitchentown Window, what happened to you?" Graham took a step back to try and examine Mike's hobbling frame.

Graham quickly got a chair and motioned for Mike to sit. He handed Mike a glass of water and placed a fan in front of the dripping container to cool him down. Then Graham placed a reassuring hand on Mike's shoulder.

"They came, see. They came and when I wouldn't let them in, they burst in, flipped me upside down, and shook me half-empty!" Mike huffed out.

Graham took his hand off Mike's shoulder and finally noticed it was covered in yellow goop. There were yellow splatters everywhere: the floor, the antiques, and now Graham. The strong smell of turmeric hung in the air, hitting Graham right in the face almost making him retch.

Detective Crackery began to feel a crack-up coming down the pike. He could see Marsha's face as she fell, he could see every gruesome crime he'd come across in his career. He didn't know if he could hold it together much longer.

Graham spit-fired a million questions at an already shell-shocked Mustardereli, each question increasing in volume:

"Are you okay? What happened? Why didn't you call the CHEESE? A Hambulance? Anything!?"

The panicked detective needed to take a deep breath. Take in the sights and smells – remain calm and figure this out. Closing his eyes, he breathed slowly and placed a warm hand on Mike's wound, "You're going to be just fine, it'll be okay. Now, what did they take?"

Mike's hand then slowly pointed to the corner of the room before he leaned over and breathed his last.

"No! Come back! Talk to me! Mike!" Graham shouted then only saw white-hot anger. His feeling of failing rushed up inside of him and Graham's temper took over. He could feel his insides screaming to get out and started using antiques to smash up other antiques.

Graham felt the spray of clay pots shattering across glass cases onto his front, not even bothering to shield himself from raining shards. His arms ached as he picked up a bookcase to smash it to the ground. Before long, he could feel his face getting red hot with rage and realized his error. He stood with his guilt and with unfathomable energy where anger just fell.

After the room was properly smashed up, Graham stood there, breathing heavily, like a Candy-Boxer standing over his beaten and broken opponent. He was wracked with emotion over the loss of his new friend and the smashed-up store due to his inability to calm down.

Mike's outstretched hand was still pointing towards the plaque that seemed to be shining brighter than anything else in the room. Through the clouds of dust clearing, Graham could make out the words:

<u>The Peppercorn Pipe:</u>
<u>The Original, Sacred Relic discovered by the founder of</u>
<u>Kitchentown, Grover Grapesmith.</u>

<u>Worth:</u>

One Fortune Cookie

Chapter Four: The Past Bites Back

ike's Rare Monuments and Other Strings lived up to half of its name after the destructive Detective was through with it. It was in such disarray, finding any subtle clues were out of the picture at this point, thanks to an unusually angry 'Crack-up.'

'Don't Crack Up,' became Crackery's mantra – a phrase that CHEESE Investigators would later learn could have saved them a lot of trouble.

Graham sat down and opened yet another candy cane, this particular one aimed to help him focus, Cocoa was a creative chemist when it came to canes.

Graham took five deep breaths in and out. He felt the tension releasing from his tightened muscles. He'd learned a few other tricks in his time as a detective that would be good for him at this moment, "Name five animal crackers at the zoo," he whispered softly to himself.

Naming each animal kept his mind sharp and farther from any intrusive panicked thoughts or feelings. He named them each methodically, eyes narrowed in the room, focusing on the issue at hand, not the issues that were plaguing him. "Giraffe. Gorilla. Lion. Tiger. Bear." he signed a big deep breath and relaxed, "Oh my. Now, where was I?"

After resetting himself, he zeroed in on a dust cloud, swirling from the aftermath of Hurricane Crackery.

Awed, Graham's candy cane almost fell out of his mouth when he noticed where the dust bowl was heading. Graham carefully made his way toward the fallen bookcase on the far wall of the room that revealed ripped wallpaper that haphazardly covered a not-so-hidden doorway.

Casually, hands rested coolly in his jacket pockets, the detective switched the cane from one side of his mouth to the other and clicked his tongue.

He stepped over the case and into the darkened, cavernous secret room. Carefully and for the first time in a long time, the dejected detective was ready and set to work.

Graham approached a computer, dimly glowing in the far corner of the mysterious office. Like a tractor bean sucking him in, Crackery almost ignored his surroundings of the other rarest of other rare items loosely decorating the room. As he approached the monitor, Graham noticed a rotating display of various boats from *Yachts by Yucca* as the screensaver vanished with the flick of the mouse.

Graham scooted the chair away from the cluttered desk. Pieces of random math equations appeared, scribbled haphazardly across every scrap of paper in sight. On the screen was a mocking, blinking cursor in the search bar of Chewgle.

Before Graham could double-click the "c" in Yucca's Yachts, a history of images and prices popped on the screen.

Noticing several of the scribbled notes matched up with the numbers on the screen, the determined detective followed the number trail up to the top.

One Fortune Cookie.

Searching through the history further, Graham began talking to himself, continuing to calm himself the best way he could, his own dialogue.

"This pipe couldn't possibly be worth a fortune cookie. Or worth that much trouble for Mike…" Graham froze.

In the recently closed tabs, there was a login already pre-typed into the Alltaste Insurance website. Graham took a big gulp before continuing to find what he feared he would stumble across – Mike Musterdareli could be a cold, stone-ground thief.

The questions loomed in his head, 'Did Mabel know? Mike and Mabel had only been dating a few months and I'd spent a few good nights in Downtown Fridgeville with both of them, who was fooling who?'

Compartmentalization had been another old trick of Graham's that he decided to dust off tonight. "Move those questions to the back of the ol' Cookie Jarhead and focus on the job," he said out loud to an echoing room. He decided to ignore anything that wasn't about the pipe and pressed on reading the clues out loud.

"Blah, blah, blah, policy change for The Precious Pipe. Boilerplate, boilerplate, yadda yadda, one fortune cookie, aha!" This was what Crackery had been searching for, "Taken out in the name of one, Salvitore Minelli."

Sirens began screeching louder in the distance; Detective Crackery only had so much time before the CHEESE arrived and stunk up the place. Graham took out his hardroll-drive and downloaded the policy.

"Whoever this Sal Minelli food is killed Mike, forged documents in his name and I WILL find out why!" muttered Graham through gritted teeth, almost cracking the hardroll drive in his fist in two.

Graham pulled out his Cracker Phone and snapped a few pictures of the scribbled notes on the desk and screen shots of Yachts and prices for evidence. More questions came to him, this time, they were relevant and helpful to the case:

"How did Mike know this Minelli character? Were they working together? Who actually owns this building? Are the Gummy's fronting another expired ex-condiment?"

Graham went to replace the chair to its proper home and almost fell back when he noticed what he'd brushed aside when he first stormed in. The intruding object slumped to the ground, along with Graham's jaw.

"...Slyvester's...vest...?"

The befuddled detective was taken aback: "What was this doing here?"

Piecing things together, Graham, pacing in a heated circle around the vest in the chair as if it was on a pedestal. The detective began to unravel the verbal and proverbial string.

"The night Marsha disappeared," Graham sat down, un-wrapped another cane and quickly continued, very aware of the sirens blaring ever closer, "It was the same night Sylvester told me where I could find that dolt, Zucchini Bellini, that got himself kidnapped. That rotten gourd couldn't have BEEN more useless that night." Graham felt his temper rising.

He decidedly named five animal crackers to calm down, quickly tidied up the room and deleted browsing history cookies. He then dusted away any crumbs of his fingerprints. Lastly, the discerning detective put on the vest and out of the office into the wall just in time to stand the bookcase back up, blocking the view of the side room.

"Detective' Crack-up, what're you doin' here?" mocked the

hulking Lieutenant Gouda.

Graham, unintimidated (or trying not to show it) slapped the CHEESE officer on the back in a friendly, yet commanding fashion, "Afternoon, Gouda. Just making sure I actually get some clues before you and your team of CHEESE-heads mess everything up. By the way, does it stink in here, or is it just you?"

Facing the cold, mean stare of the CHEESE Officer, Graham held his smile and began to walk out with a casual wave, "Later CHEESE-ball!"

6

Chapter Five: InVestigation

I t was dark by the time Graham boarded the K-train from Mike's back to downtown Kitchentown and his own crumby apartment. Graham decided his work was finished for the day; he'd uncovered enough information and needed to digest this new, potentially devastating breakthrough.

Plus, Mike was gone. Graham's new friend, just taken from him.

Today was heavy and the detective needed to rest his weary soul. His dreams, however, were not in agreement.

'Graham, hold me,' whispered Marsha, facing away from Graham in bed. She was having another law school nightmare.

Graham rolled over to provide some comfort from whatever was haunting her dreams.

Graham gingerly placed a hand on her side, letting her know all would be okay and as he stared into her eyes, deeply. Without warning, her skin became sticky and began melting into the bed.

"Marsha?!" recoiled Graham, not having a clue how to handle his sweetheart oozing away from him.

"Graham, helbbbbppppp," her lips started drooping off to the side as she started disappearing at an increasingly rapid pace. Oozing off the bed, Marsha began pouring into a drain on the floor of Graham's room until all he could hear was the muffled calls for help.

"Grmmmmm!"

Scrambling to open the drain, he nearly broke his fingers trying to pry up the grate. As Graham reached for a screwdriver, his other hand started crumbling, making it impossible to get a grip on anything.

Crackery tried to stand to get help but his soft legs gave out underneath him, crumbling along with her. He was falling apart; she was melting away. He reached out,

"Marsha, no!"

His entire body fell to pieces on the floor until he saw a dark shadow over him. The last thing he heard was a sneering, familiar voice:

"Suns comin' up, bub. Get up before that yellow ball rises."

Graham shot up and awoke in a puddle of icing. Breathing heavily, he figured he'd be used to the nightmares at this point.

Graham knew he wouldn't get over Marsha anytime soon but at least these nightmares should slowly come to a halt.

And now this new, harsh element, a terrifying and familiar voice, but Detective Crackery needed to shake it off and keep his head clear.

Graham knew he needed to pay a visit to the last place he wanted to be today:

The CHEESE station.

Crackery needed more info on Mike's death and the newly found vest.

The Detective arrived in the frigid hallways of the morgue. Located deep underneath the CHEESE Station where the detective had previously had to do some of the dirtiest detective work of his career. Graham had identified thousands of missing labels, pointed out pickles that passed the point of expiration, and viewed charred remains of several grill deals gone bad.

This time was different. This wasn't just another situation gone bad in Kitchentown; this was Mike Mustardereli — Graham's jovial and quirky friend. Mike had a life short-lived in Kitchentown and Graham would avenge it any way he could.

Taking one last look at Graham's empty bottle-shaped buddy, he decided to say a quick send-off, "See ya on the other side of the Big Window, Mike. You'll be missed."

Graham pulled his hat down over his face to cover a single streaming tear as he walked back out into the hallway.

Although he was mourning the loss of a friend, something

about the empty shell that used to be Mike didn't look right –
changed, but somehow *too* different.

Then again, nothing felt quite right anymore.

After leaving his emptied friend, Graham walked into the
hallway to a waiting Captain Bleu. The last time he was in the
CHEESE station, the night Sylvester disappeared and Marsha
melted, Graham started a fight with nearly every stinking piece
of CHEESE in the building.

Blame and broken desks were hurled. Slammed into walls
and plaques not-so-delicately smashed into faces of CHEESE
officers that tried to get near the uncontrollable Cracked-Up
Graham Crackery.

He didn't take loss too well and it unfortunately showed all
over the station. Several officers were taken out of the building
on stretchers, others had chunks that were no longer attached
to their frames — it was a queso bath. And one that Graham
regretted causing.

One that would haunt him for a long time to come.

Thankfully, Bleu had a soft spot for Graham. He knew that
Graham was able to do more CHEESE work in a day than his
officers could do in a week.

It took all of Bleu's connections to have the case against
Graham, and his crack-up dropped. Bleu gave a pass to the
devastated detective that night. Marsha was lost to save an
ungrateful Zucchini Bellini, and all while having to deal with the
Gummy's continually pestering Graham week in and week out.

"I was sorry to hear about Mike, Detective. He was a great
guy and full of gusto," said the oldest CHEESE on the force and
soon-to-retire Old Bleu.

Roquefort M. Bleu, the first honest CHEESE of Police to protect
Kitchentown. He ran the city the way it should have been run,

with care and empathy, which kept Kitchentown fresh.

Over the years young Bleu slowly crumbled into Old Bleu and the city declined from integrity to simply gritty. Graham was able to find a mentor amongst what little good Bleu had left. Bleu was the father Graham never had. But, after the Crack-Up and all Bleu had done to get the detective away from trouble, their relationship had gotten moldy. Bleu's reputation took a nose dive along with Graham's after that.

"Thanks, Chief." Graham hardly acknowledged the condolences before robotically moving on, desperate to change the subject, "Almost done with Kitchentown, huh pal?

"Only if it's done with me," Bleu grumbled gruffly.

"There is one more thing." Graham handed over Slyvester's vest with the Peppercorn Pipe's ransom letter on top.

"I need to know where this letter came from and if it's related to this vest in any way."

Bleu took the items from Graham. "I'll let you know when I know anything. Take care of yourself, detective."

They shook hands and Graham left, feeling the weight of the vest and the letter, off his chest.

He needed time to process the loss of Mike and the uncomfortable conversation he'd need to have with Mike's girlfriend, Mabel.

That would be tomorrow's problem.

One of Graham's problems was his ability to procrastinate when things got too unpleasant. It would always be tomorrow and tomorrow and tomorrow. He knew tonight would be filled with nightmares and he needed to prepare. Candy canes were aplenty, but rest went wanting, once again.

Graham wiped the nonstop assault of water from his face as he climbed to the top of the soon-to-open Sink Resort's main attraction:

The Dehydrator Spa.

The continuous construction allowed for Graham to get to the top quickly, thanks to a few strategically placed ladders and several red-vine ropes. Graham maneuvered quickly through the obstacle course-like layout and arrived at the open maw of the Dehydrator, the rush of the sink ever-present.

Initially marketed as a steamy and relaxing opening weekend for all Veggiekind in Kitchentown, today it proved the failure had turned deadly. The Dehydrator continued to malfunction thanks to the poorly planned location and the rains from the sink which were unusually heavy this time of night.

The city had never fully inspected the plans to have a waterfall in close proximity to a deadly caldron of heat and electricity. As always, there was too much money to be made from the prime-rib real estate.

Another bad construction job in Kitchentown, another fat payday for the Gummy Family. It was the very same death trap that Zucchini Bellini, heir of the Bellini Media Corporation was swinging over. Bound and gagged, Zucchini's limp body swung helplessly above the heated cauldron. He was way too close to being cooked for good.

"I'm coming, Zuch!" yelled Graham over the roar of the sink as he climbed closer and reached out. Whoever turned up the sink that evening wasn't playing around and they certainly weren't stupid; they knew what they were doing.

The plan made Graham sick to his stomach: use some aristocarrot's kid as leverage. Lure the detective to a dangerous situation and hopefully remove Graham from any equation going forward.

The Gummy's had no soul in the soft underbelly of their large belly.

Graham's thoughts immediately became interrupted by fate.

"Graham, I'm coming!" shouted a familiar, soft voice below him.

Before he even turned around, Crackery knew that sweet voice, making his heart sink.

"Why did you follow me?" was the last thing he would say to the love of his life.

Marsha's normally nimble frame slipped off of the red vines and into the dark of the Dehydrator. Graham shot his hand out, reaching for Marsha, only to feel her hand skim his, ever so softly for only a second before it was gone.

7

Chapter Six: Mabel's Sticky Situation

The Kitchentown Crier arrived while Graham was bathing in the rejuvenating warmth of his frosting shower. He didn't hear the paper hit his door, but the impact would affect him, nonetheless.

A fresh cup of coco-coffee in hand, the ill-prepared detective picked up the paper and read it. He was still preparing himself to visit the author of the article that was slapped across the front page:

Precious Peppercorn Pipe Purloined, Shop Owner Expired

The piece started out with a note to the reader, followed by what appeared to be half eulogy, half news report of a crime.

Dear Reader, it is with great sadness that I write the following article.

While some at The Crier have noted I'm too close to the story, which could taint it, others understand there is a catharsis in this writing; along with a farewell and hopefully some form of closure.

However, first and foremost, I'm a journalist and my integrity will always stand with the story over the emotions behind it. Thank you for understanding and staying with me in these trying times. –Mabel S.

Graham's coco-coffee had gone cold as he read the opening of the article a few times, feeling Mabel's sadness with each word. He read on while wiping away his own tears.

Unsure which feeling was overtaking him at the moment, Graham felt grief for Mabel.

The rest of the article focused on addressing the importance of the Pipe to those in Kitchentown. To some, the Pipe stood for the basis of their spirituality. To others, there was a strong, almost nationalistic importance that inhabited the Pipe.

Then there were those that saw the Pipe as a promise of energy for Kitchentown. Some scientists believed that peppercorns had the potential to be an enormous source of power, and the pipe was the symbol of this belief. Making the Pipe itself priceless.

Whoever stole the Pipe was well aware of the impact it would have on the town and potentially their bank accounts.

What most Foodkind learned in school about the Pipe was its discovery by the Founder of Kitchentown, Grover Grapesmith.

The real history of the Pipe was it was stolen from the Black Pepparians, the first inhabitants of Kitchentown before it was a town, before Dairyville, and before it was taken over by Grover's family and friends.

It was an oasis and The Pepparians were nothing to sneeze at.

However, the Grapesmith family had bigger plans for this paradise and were able to overtake the simple nature and free-spirited Pepparians, all but ridding the countryside of them.

Finally, the article (omitting most of the real history of the Pipe) ended with a heartfelt tribute to Mike Mustardereli and the inevitable closure and the auctioning off of items within Mike's Rare Monuments and Other Strings.

Mabel and Mike had only been dating a short time but her writing led the readers to believe they were star-crossed lovers, two peas in a pod, sandwiched together forever.

When the detective arrived at Mabel's loft, he was hardly able to knock before Mabel swung open the door, as if she knew it was him.

"I wondered what took you so long to visit," Mabel said warmly to Graham as they embraced each other for comfort.

Mabel and Graham had been through the ringer the last few months. Each losing their significant other to an awful crime, neither having any answers.

"Mabel, I'm so sorry for your loss," Graham struggled to say, looking down while holding his hat as if he was embarrassed to be in her presence.

"Honestly, Graham," she lightly touched his face and brought it to look up at her sympathetic face.

"We weren't that close. Not like you and Marsha were. Sorry if that's too soon."

Graham was taken aback by the news and hearing Marsha's name so bluntly hurled at him. Regaining his composure, he made a note of Mabel's truth-stretching exercises in her article about the nature of her relationship with Mike. He pressed on, "You were both so..." Graham struggled for the word, "So, compatible."

Mabel shrugged off the comment and motioned for the detective to remove his bread shoes and follow her back to her office. She lived in Sporks, one of the freshest Drawer Buildings in Kitchentown. Her loft overlooked the busy intersection of Forker St and Spoony Blvd, a helpful view in her line of work.

Graham followed her back while stepping over boxes of documents from her years of writing various stories and reports. The hallways were lined with article headlines about Mabel's prowess as a short story writer. A shrine to a bygone era, left in the cookie dust for bigger and more important things.

Strewn about her desk were several crumbled-up cashed checks from short story contests that had been entered and won. She always felt she should earn money from telling the truth, not silly little fictions.

Ms. Seerup was never one to care about fame or notoriety, she used to write stories as a means to an end. At first, Mabel felt a sense of connection to her favorite author, F. Scott Fudgegerald. She would write these stories to fund her true passion of journalism. An expensive direction to take in life, but a noble cause and one she had a strong talent for.

"Mike and I were somewhat compatible, sure, but happy? Notsomuch," Mabel mentioned almost in passing as she sat down at her desk across from the wary sleuth. He couldn't help but notice several 'Final Notice' bills on her desk, all from her time at Chardvard University.

"Yea, those are never going away." She smiled, "You'd think after all I've done to help Kitchentown, I'd get a break." Mabel noticed Graham eyeballing her mail. "Turns out the Gummy's pay well, but writing about their crimes? Also, notsomuch," she remarked offhandedly, grabbing as many bills as she could handle and tossing them in a messy drawer.

Another odd comment and behavior went into Graham's mental notepad for later.

Maybe she grieved in her own way and in her own time, but her coldness about Mike's passing and this sea of debt Mabel swam in crept on Graham's detective radar aggressively.

Mabel's tone seemed to shift from indifference to caring in an instant, almost as if she sensed his suspicions.

"I'm still worried about you, Graham. After Marsha, Mike and I both felt like you weren't the same Crackery we knew. I felt bad I never contacted you after she...well. You know."

Graham got up and walked away from her view. He felt the need to hide his tears, but he also used this time as an excuse to do a little investigating. Maybe there were some remnants of Mike that could help. Mabel seemed to have already cleared most of Mike out of her apartment. No pieces of mail with his name, no belongings, not even a picture of them.

Graham cleared his throat and responded, "How often did Mike stay over here?"

Brushing off the question, Mabel pressed on her own conversation, "You know I thought the world of Marsha. She was crushing it as the District Attorney working hand in hand with Mayor Naise to clean up this town."

As Mabel mentioned the Mayor's name, Graham's hue changed to a dark red, his fists became clenched.

Throughout the last few days, she forgot how much the very mention of the Mayor would make Graham upset. There was always tension between Graham and the Mayor over Marsha.

Mabel quickly changed the subject and nearly avoided a crack-up.

"Together, her and I felt like we were cleaning up large sections of Kitchentown. She would leak just the right amount of information to help lead the public to rally behind true justice."

Reading Graham's feelings of being left out, she tossed him a bone.

"Detective, you were always there to step in and give the CHEESE the evidence they needed in half the time it took the CHEESE to even begin the investigation. We all did a lot of good together. We just never could quite get to the meat and potatoes of the crime syndicate; those rotten Gummy's."

Graham knew this wasn't just pandering to help make him feel better, she was right: Marsha and Mabel were truly a dynamic duo curbing crime in Kitchentown.

Neighborhoods were finally being swept up, which allowed families to safely enjoy the outdoors again; they were able to get to know their neighbors again and build back their communities.

The Gummy's, feeling deserted yet undetered, were always looking for ways to muck up Kitchentown and had, thanks to Marsha and Mabel, decided to turn to more subtle and less savory ways of baking Kitchentown for all it was worth.

Mabel hesitated, starting and stopping what she was about to say to Graham, unsure how he would take it. "I'm scared,

Detective."

She was right, Graham was struck by her unusually frank confession. He began looking at Mabel in a couple different ways and now Graham needed Cocoa to springboard his thoughts on what was happening.

"How can I help?" offered Graham, hesitantly, unsure just what frightened someone who wrote about the worst of the worst in Kitchentown.

Mabel shifted in her seat, unable to look Graham in the eyes, "They went after Mike to get what they wanted and now he's gone. What if I'm next?

He used to tell me a lot about his business; where the safe was, the combination, and everything. We had a lot of trust between us. Not really happiness, but for some reason, he told me a lot about a lot. If his expirationers know about me, am I safer than Mike's safe?"

What DOES she actually know? thought Graham to himself.

"There's something else," Mabel hesitated, "I can't find my recorder. Marsha and I kept records of all of our meetings; it was our insurance."

Graham was struck by the odd use of the word, 'insurance.' He fought off any additional intrusive 'what ifs' as his Cracker Phone rang.

'Saved by the lunch bell.' he thought before answering. He looked at Mabel before starting the call.

"Don't worry, I'll keep an ear out for it." Then answered his phone.

"Hello? You don't say?"

Mabel looked up at Graham concerned with what news was coming on the other line. Graham's urgency climbed with each response.

"You don't say?" Another long pause, then, "Okay, I'll be right there."

"What did they say?" Mabel almost whispered.

"They didn't." Graham replied matter-of-factly, and quickly left.

8

Chapter Seven: Next Steps

Graham felt shaken but not stirred. He didn't want to just up and leave Mabel in that condition, but he wasn't exactly sure what condition he was leaving her in.

"How truthful was she actually being?" He thought as he walked.

"She swore allegiance to the truth, but seemingly less so these last few days, apparently."

Besides, the results for the vest and letter were in.

Graham had promised Bleu if he needed something to call the mainline and use a different voice, it would be too suspicious to the rest of the unit if Graham kept calling directly.

Unfortunately, CHEESE Labs couldn't disclose any information over Graham's Cracker Phone. The detective needed to reach out to the investigator who had the results. Going to the station would be the fastest way to gain the information but calling them and dialing through the automated system for a bit was the lesser of two evils.

Closing his eyes, Graham sat, losing himself in a memory while listening to the on-hold music chiming over the phone.

"If you like Pina Coladas..."

"and getting caught in the grain!" sang Marsha as she entered Graham's study.

Graham looked up from his case file and smiled at this welcome intrusion.

"What are you so happy about today?" smiled Graham.

Marsha struck a pose as she related her incredible news, "You're looking at the new District Attorney for Kitchentown!"

Graham literally tossed his work aside and jumped up in joy as they held each other in a warm and celebratory embrace – continuously jumping up and down in excitement.

"So, what's next, what does this mean for you? Besides notoriety,

fame, and all the good stuff you deserve." Graham fawned.

Marsha turned away and hesitated. Graham had always been her biggest fan and supporter, but this would be a tough pill for him to swallow.

"I'll be working directly in the Hellman Building..." she trailed off.

Graham's smile froze and dropped, "With Mayor Naise?"

Marsha continued on, "Yup, Jordan and I will be taking on some of the top crimes in Kitchentown, maybe even some cases with the Gummy's."

Detective Crackery's insides were all over the place. He felt pride for Marsha and her well-deserved accomplishments. He also felt pangs of jealousy and anger knowing the Mayor would be near her more often.

"Jordan," repeated Graham sarcastically with a fragment of anger coming through, "is someone I've been investigating for a long time in connection to a lot of bad stuff that goes on in Kitchentown."

Marsha knew what came next, she'd heard this speech a baker's dozen times when she was in Law School and interning.

While Graham paced and ranted, she silently mouthed along, "I mean, he comes from a long line of corruption, since that rotten Hellmann Building was inhabited by Naise."

"So, there's no additional congratulations coming? No celebrations? It's all about the Mayor?" Marsha crossed her arms out of justified frustration – this was her day to enjoy, not his to ruin.

Graham shook his head and smiled.

"You're right, my sweetness. Let's head over to our BBQ spot. I'm pretty sure I'll need to borrow a napkin or two from you." He grinned.

Marsha softened and stepped into Graham's arms. She looked up into his loving eyes, he looked back – they were caught in the tractor bean of love.

She opened her mouth to whisper sweet nothings, but all that came out was a gruff voice of a CHEESE officer.

"It's on, Graham. Detective? Are you there?"

Graham snapped back to reality.

"It turned on, Graham. Did you hear me? Detective? Hello? Something in the vest you gave us turned on."

While Graham's stomach flipped upside down, defying gravity, Bleu delivered the news to the now-understanding Crackery. For a second he felt like the floor was going to give out underneath him. Bleu's voice continued.

"We think it's a microphone or a camera, or something. We need to know where you found this, and Graham..."

The pause left the detective speechless.

"There's something else on it as well."

Graham froze, waiting.

"The micro-lab found a fragment from a paper that looks like a business card. The point of origin came from," Bleu held back to pause for dramatic effect.

"The Hellman Building. Detective, please listen before you hang up..."

Graham rushed out of his office, barely remembering to lock up before leaving.

He needed to talk to Cocoa. He couldn't have a Crack-Up in front of the Mayor, but anger was floating on Graham's surface. He decided to ring Cocoa and fill him in on Mabel and this new vest clue springing up, seeing what his companion could offer in advice or thoughts.

"Cocoa, it's Graham, listen; I'm about to do something really bone-headed, got a minute?"

Chapter Eight: Dairyville

After Graham filled Cocoa in on the last few details he recovered, he could feel Cocoa's apologetic tone come through his Cracker Phone.

"Graham, you know I'm here for you no matter what, but the timing couldn't be worse. I'm actually checking out this awesome location near your office for my Candy Canes store, Cocoa's Canes! I'm doing a walk through now, but call me after you speak with Jordan and I'll see how I can help."

The downtrodden detective felt flushed but understood Cocoa needed his own time and his own life.

"No, it's all good, Cocoa, you deserve this! I'll keep you posted. Good luck!" replied Graham.

"Hey bud, do me a favor," Cocoa's tone grew more serious.

"When you speak to the Mayor, take it easy. Try and remember you have a job to do. And he also lost someone."

Annoyed by Cocoa's correct answer, Graham hung up. He knew the Mayor lost a DA, and the first non-corrupt one Kitchentown had seen in a long time.

The breadstick benches were usually empty outside of Graham's office. The row of seats was a ghost town, enabling Graham to catch some fresh air outside of his office while not having to interact with anyone. Today, Graham needed the opposite, he needed a soundboard and knew that Cocoa was fading in that area.

The detective sat down on the benches and tried to think. He closed his eyes, but nothing came. He needed the back and forth with someone, but who?

Before he could reopen his eyes, a slight weight shift on his bench, and a small shadow appeared over Graham. He shot his eyes open to see the diminutive Artie Chokerode sitting next to him, "Hiya Detective Crackery, need some help?"

Graham Crackery, for better or for worse, struggled with letting people in after Marsha's accident; Artie was no exception. He didn't want this innocent little stalk to get injured or worse.

By all accounts in Kitchentown, Arite Chockerode was wasting her time behind the taxi wheel. She was cool, whip-smart, and as personable as one could get.

Throughout her time driving Food to and from everywhere, she learned all the routes necessary for a potential getaway. She got to know the ins and outs of Dairyville and the comings and goings outside of the Hellman Building. The map of Kitchentown seemed to be imprinted in her brain, which made her the eyes and ears of every Food in Kitchentown. Graham could certainly use an extra pair of each at the moment.

"Alright, let's do this, I'll explain on the way. Let's head over to the Hellman Building." Graham stood up and walked towards the backdoor of the cab. As Graham rounded the back of the car Artie was already standing with the door open as wide as the smile on her face.

"You won't regret this. How can I help?" asked Artie excitedly as she hopped in the driver's seat, buckled herself in, and took off.

The drive to The Fridge was short but the traffic in and around Dairyville and the Hellman Building was extra thick today. This gave Graham enough time to fill in what's been going on and bounce some ideas off of Artie.

In the middle of the detective blandly running through his case notes, Artie interjected.

"I have to ask, detective, you seem like you're holding back. What's up?"

Graham stopped, not expecting such an intrusive question

from someone he didn't know very well. Before Graham could respond, Artie continued forcefully.

"Look, we both know that my dad had business with..."

The detective regained his voice and interrupted, "We don't have to talk about that."

"Actually, detective, we do. I want to help, I know you walk by me all the time when you could just stop and ask, but you don't!"

Artie was chipper, but not taking no for an answer. Her tactic usually resulted in changing most 'no's' to 'yes'.

Graham huffed, the taxi wasn't going anywhere. They were wedged in pumpkin-to-pumpkin traffic.

"Look, your dad was the head engineer that helped build The Dehydrator. No offense, but it was built poorly and Marsha's not in my life anymore because of it."

"Feel better now?" chuffed Artie. "What you don't know is that night you protected my family years ago from the Gummy's. Well, they came to attack my father after you'd gone." Graham sat quietly, saddened by this new information.

"He wouldn't lower his standards for them to save costs." Artie proudly reported to Graham.

"They...they took him. We don't know where he is or if he's alive." Artie tried to wipe away a single tear stealthily, but the detective was all too aware.

"The Gummy's took him on his way home from the Stalkton Heights Plant, the night the Bellini kid was rescued, you were a little busy."

Artie, losing patience and formality continued, "Detective, they distracted you with a high-profile kidnapping. Then took my father, someone that wouldn't get a lot of attention in the Panini Press if he went missing. It worked! No one talks about him anymore, but all the Tea-V did was go on and on about how Zuch was returned safely."

Graham felt sorrow for Artie and her family.

"I'm sorry about your dad. And I've been avoiding your help, which I could use right now. I promise, after this, we'll find your father together too, deal?" Graham reached his arm out and shook Artie's while they sat inching ever closer to the Hellman Building.

"Back to business." Artie felt cool as a cucumber. She didn't want to be too obvious, especially at the opportunity to find her missing father. At least she hoped he was only missing, it could be worse.

Putting the negativity out of her mind, she pressed on, ready for adventure.

"What's waiting for us at the Hellman?" Artie abbreviated, like providing a fun nickname, hoping to further put their past behind them while binding them together.

They discussed the letter along with Sylvester's vest, most of which Artie interjected Graham's story with what she'd read in the Kitchentown Crier. She would then repeat herself. "Sorry, I just love Mabel Seerup's reporting, she's a great writer."

Graham responded with a sly smile, "I couldn't agree more. Maybe you can tell her yourself?"

Artie didn't know that her smile could get any bigger than it had been.

Graham laid out the plan as they got closer to their destination.

"When we get in there, let's just play it cool. Pretend to be a little slow with the Mayor. We need him to think we're just asking questions because we don't have any information." Graham's plans tended to center around his impulsivity.

"Mapped out plans always involve a degree of thinking you have

control over an environment that's uncontrollable. Let the moment guide you." Bleu used to say when Graham was learning the red vine ropes of being a detective.

"*Be able to improvise.*"

Graham verbally laid out the puzzle for Artie, hoping the Mayor would fill in a couple of missing pieces.

"We know the letter had fragments on it that were also found on Sylvestor's vest. Those microscopic specs have originated from the Mayor's office. He's our main suspect, but we can't let him know that we're on to him." Graham instructed.

Artie pulled into a spot close to the Hellman Building entrance and turned to Graham. "Are you ready for this?"

Graham smiled. He loved that energy.

Cocoa was a great soundboard, but Artie's positivity and enthusiasm was infectious. It gave Graham the motivation he needed to get past the emotions of the case. Graham stepped out of the cab and looked down at Artie, "We need to be careful. There's a lot of sacred history here." Artie nodded along and agreed, "It's important to walk on eggshells near this building."

Dairyville was the cream of the crop in The Fridge. Vast open spaces and crazy night-life helped it become one of the wealthiest residential townchips in Kitchentown. Here, at The Fridge, the heart of it all was also home to The Hellman Building and the office of Mayor Naise.

When Dairyville was founded, The Hellman's came in with ideas of massive growth. What had once been places of serenity for another founding family, the Butterfields', were being demolished daily. The first Mayor Mansion of Kitchentown to reside in Dairyville would be where they took over Butter Tree Park unaware and uncaring of the impact such destruction would amount to.

Much like the squabbles of Kitchentown's origins, during the foundation of Dairyville, there was fierce competition as to who the real founders were, The Hellman's or the Butterfield's.

The Butterfields and the Hellmann's were sworn enemies. Forked into a constant battle thanks in part to the unwavering pride of the Butterfields and the unmatched greed and immorality of the Hellmann's.

They'd arrived in Kitchentown through the Great Window around the same time as Grover Grapesmith laid down land outside of the Fridge.

The Butterfields saw Dairyville as a souptopia. A place where all could come together in one big melting pot and grow the city and their community up around them. A community built with respect and, happily, one that would have made Detective Crackery's job unnecessary.

One Ice-cream floats all boats was the official slogan for the Butterfield campaign and their pledge to lead Dairyville for the Groceries and Food; Equality for all.

The Hellman's, however, came in with a radically different idea. Bully the locals, teaming up with the Grapesmiths to take over land that wasn't theirs. Paving paradise and building up an explosion of lights and colors.

Buildings, unnecessary attractions, and plenty of distractions. A smoke and mirrors spectacle to entice Kitchentown into a stupor while the Hellmann's, and eventually the Naise's would rob them blind through their connections in government. It was as if the Gummy's had borrowed right from their playbook and teamed up to take over the town.

The Butterfields didn't stand a chance thanks in part to their stubbornness in refusing to play dirty like their competition.

Playing by the rules eventually just meant you're stuck in your own prison created by those that played by their own rules.

The Fridge began to grow into a larger, more modern part of Kitchentown. Building it up from mini to large Fridge, Dairyville quickly became the Capital with the Hellman Building at its center rack.

Kitchentown, for all of its splendor still had to deal with the unfortunate reality of its inception: The Grapesmiths and the Hellman's had bested the Butterfields and the Pepparians. Equality for all would take a backseat to those who had the dough and more importantly, the influence.

Today was incidentally a celebrated holiday in Dairyville, Grocery Day, which some in the Hellman Building referred to as the year in which the town was founded.

That meant The Fridge was going to be packed in with vast crowds of patriotic Foods. Artie almost lost Graham amongst all of the commotion:

A field trip of young Dumplings poured out of one tour bus, each one excitedly lined up to get into the main hall of the Hellmann Building for a long-anticipated school trip.

A group of milkmen and women, close to their expiration date, come in to pay some innocuous bill or argue with the town committee about a new traffic cream cone, simply out of sheer boredom.

The slowness of these groups impeding the detective's work started to make Graham's better mood sour. The detective tried his best to keep his cool and not get mad or yell out. After all, they just wanted one final tour or day out before gently going into that good bite.

After what felt like an eternity of waiting and wading through the sea of Food around them; Artie grabbed Graham's hand and began pushing through the crowd to the front of the West Chicken Wing: Mayor Jordan Naise's residence.

10

Chapter Nine: Mayor Naise Spreads Lies

Roberta 'Bobbi' Cottage was standing behind Mayor Naise as he sat at his desk. She'd grown accustomed to this practice while they edited a big speech. Jordan was preparing to deliver remarks regarding the rampant inflation in Kitchentown on this auspicious holiday. He wanted to address the town about rising yeasts and how those costs can affect them plus what he was going to do about it.

Bobbi and Jordan had been friends since they were half pints, and growing up together gave Bobbi an insight into the Naise household that many would never see.

She understood where Jordan came from, and more importantly, that his namesake was his unfortunate and inevitable downfall. Jordan didn't like the image his family projected; one day he'd vowed to fix it at any cost.

Even if that involved leaning into the corruption of the Naise family as a means to become Mayor and actually do some real cleaning up in Kitchentown.

"Sir, if you mention inflation too strongly, the audience's eyes dry up. You need to keep them engaged in other issues. Kitchentown-table issues." added Bobbi to a clearly stressed-out Mayor.

"I hear you. You mentioned that, it's just..." he hesitated. "You know how Food in the Fridge can be. One minute you're top shelf and one wrong word pushes you to the back. Easily forgotten."

Jordan was showing his rare true self to his only confidant. He knew the polls weren't rising in his favor lately, no matter how many Gummy's had expired.

The intercom interrupted their conflict for the moment as the Mayor's secretary, Steve Stalkton, buzzed through the speaker.

"Sir, there's a Detective Crackery and, what was your name,

sweetheartichoke?" Asked the heir to Stalkton Heights to an annoyed Artie.

"The name is Artie Chokerode and we're a little behind schedule. Why don't you move aside your game of Solipear, it's blocking your boss' calendar. We clearly called ahead, so, if you could simply open the door, that would be great." squeaked Artie sarcastically.

Silence on the other end for a moment, then the doors opened up. Steve was obviously given this job because of his name, not his talents, or tact and lack thereof.

Jordan swallowed hard. Bobbi straightened up. They both braced for a potential crack-up. Instead, Artie walked in first purposefully while Graham stared hard at the young Stalkton before slowly following, much less eager to be here. Steve didn't need Graham to utter a word to get the message, *treat all Food equally.*

Bobbi first stepped forward to greet the impromptu guests, however, before she could get around the desk, Jordan was already halfway to Graham with arms open, a mournful face, and beckoning the confused detective for a hug.

"Detective Crackery, I can't tell you how devastated I am about Marsha. I know we haven't spoken since, but how are you?" Jordan's arms were fully around Graham, whose arms were limp and half-accepting the awkward embrace.

"Well, seeing as how there's a few things missing in this town and the CHEESE isn't much help, I'm just peachy." Graham's blunt remark almost physically removed the Mayor from around the detective's waist to an awaiting Artie, her hand extended waiting for Jordan's.

"I'm Artie, let's have a seat and chat. Hi," turning now to Bobbi, "I'm Artie, nice to meat you." Graham admired her courage and ability to cut through unnecessary small talk.

The four Food in the group all politely shook hands, following Artie's lead, and had a seat in their respective chairs.

Graham and Artie sat waiting for any opening from either the Mayor or Bobbi, keeping the information about the vest, very close to their chest.

"Well," started Bobbi, "thank you for coming in, we're all clearly on edge about the missing Pipe so let's try and keep things at a cool pace."

Artie continued her role to impress Graham.

"Agreed. So, what have you learned from your internal investigation from CHEESE? I'm assuming they report to you?"

Jordan and Bobbi looked at Artie, then at each other, and back at Graham, "Is your driver here to interrogate, or can you and I speak off the record?" Jordan commented dryly.

Graham motioned towards Artie, "My associate asked you a question, it would be polite to address her. I have a few questions of my own, but I'll wait. Got any coco-coffee?"

Jordan begrudgingly hit a button and a few minutes later Steve awkwardly stumbled through the doorway with two coco-coffee's for the unwelcome guests, bowing in uncomfortable reverence on his way out.

"Anything else?" offered Bobbi.

"Nope, just a few answers," quipped Arite before taking a long sip and leaving the coco-coffee untouched for the rest of the meeting.

Jordan sighed and continued, "Look, there are things I can share, and things I simply can't."

He paused for another moment and continued, voice lowered more this time.

"We believe that Mike was somehow involved with the Gummy

family. We have documents to show they hired him to run his store. The Gummy's weren't aware just how astutely Mike had a real knack for knick-knacks.

When they realized the possession he'd acquired, they wanted it at all costs and 86'd Mike for the prized Pipe." Jordan sat back and waited for any reaction.

"You learned this through the mold in the CHEESE station, I'm assuming?" Graham quickly asked.

Jordan sat frozen. Bobbi didn't blink. "How do you know about that?" Jordan asked, clearly nervous now.

Graham sat smiling, "How do *you*?" Graham knew about the mold, but not who it was. He sat in silence with an ever patient look on his face. Graham took a long sip of his coco-coffee, waiting for one of them to spill the tea.

Bobbi leaned forward, "Okay, we both know that B..."

Jordan interrupted her quickly, "Ah, that, uh... both of you are curious as to who it is so let's find an amicable way to clue you in and help me out in return."

"That's called a squid pro quo. A.K.A a big no-no in your profession, sir" Artie shot back. "Please, continue on who that mold is. We're very busy."

Graham's coco-coffee cup fell seemingly in slow motion as Bobbi said the informant's name. All the detective could hear was an increasingly louder ringing in his ears. Through blurred vision, he could see Artie waving in his face.

The detective's senses returned to hear Artie ask him again, "Who's Ol' Bleu?"

Chapter Ten: Running Out of Time

Graham's world had shattered more than a few times in the last few months. Finally, he assumed after a while he would just hit rock bottom and get used to bad news. He never did find that bottom.

Graham whispered through a dry mouth, "The CHEESE of Police."

Bobbi and Jordan both understood the relationship Graham had with Bleu. They knew how much of a mentor Bleu was to the devastated detective and how Bleu went to bat for Graham on several occasions.

Graham decided anger was no longer an emotion he had anything in the tank for. It was just blunt force truth at this point – emotionless, zero tact.

"Everything you touch smears, you know that?" Graham stood, pointing at Jordan, ready to blame him for all of the detective's problems.

"Bleu was a fine officer of the CHEESE force, now he's a mold working with you and the Gummy's." Graham paused to hold for effect before continuing.

"Marsha worked with you. She was a rising talent, and where is she now? You were getting close to Mike, where is he now?"

All of his anger and frustration had to come out, and he refused to have it be destructive physically, so he went for it emotionally instead.

"Everything you touch, smears. You and Cottage, here." pointing now to Bobbi.

"You both reek of corruption. You both reek of downfall. I will find a way to expose you."

Graham turned to walk out with Artie quickly in tow. Jordan stood up to respond, but, knowing better, Bobbi held him back and allowed Graham to leave.

Graham couldn't help but turn, and with calm resolve, throw in one final barb:

"Marsha always said the best part of the Hellman Building was the change she was able to make in a day." He paused, straightened his tie and uttered coldly, "But the worst part was the stench of mediocrity." Graham dropped the last word with authority.

That was one comment Jordan couldn't sit well with. He stood up and took one careful step forward, pointing at the detective's back as he walked away.

"*You* held Marsha back." The Mayor's finger and voice were shaking.

"She was on her way to the top but said you were always too needy."

Graham froze in the doorway but didn't turn around. Jordan kept pushing.

"Why don't you take a long walk off a short pier and go join her, detective?"

Artie quickly pushed Graham forward and out into the hustle

and bustle of Diaryville, away from continued conflict. Bobbi sat looking disappointed at The Mayor, still standing pointing at an empty room.

Artie pushed Graham in a beeline for the edge of the walkway that lined Dairyville. They both looked out over the cityscape of Fridgeville and took a few deep breaths. Graham carefully pulled out another candy cane when a familiar voice came up behind them.

"Hey man, how's it crackin'?" A confused Crackery turned around just in time for Cocoa's hat to bonk Graham squarely on the nose. His cane broke in half and fell to the ground. Graham was still in shock, his first case in over a month was cracking him at the edges.

Artie bent down and picked up Cocoa's hat, then steered both of them towards her awaiting taxi.

"Now is not the time for a crack-up, let's get him out of here," she whispered to Cocoa. He nodded as they were putting Graham in the backseat to lie down before anyone else in the crowd could notice.

This time of day, leaving Fridgeville was a lot quicker and less traffic-filled. The sun was setting outside of the Great Window, Graham was starting to doze off to the sound of Artie filling Cocoa in on the latest news from Mayor Naise and Bobbi Cottage. They could discuss all of this when they got back to the office. Now, Graham needed to rest.

The sink water was beating down hard. Graham's cast-iron grasp on Marsha's melting hand began to slip further in the heat of the Dehydrator.

"Graham, don't let me gooobpebrbrr!" shouted Marsha. Her mouth melting, her speech becoming more impossible to under-

stand.

The look of terror was quickly replaced by a subtle sweet farewell on both Graham and Marsha's faces as they looked into each other's eyes for the last time.

Graham, telling her that all will be okay with the soft look of confidence. Marsha calmly held tight, accepting her fate before slipping out of sight.

All that remained of Marsha was now stuck to Graham's hand. He stared in disbelief at the white glob that was once Marsha's small hand, now stuck in his palm.

Graham's disbelief swirling like the waterfall drenching the Sink Resort's bottom.

The Dehydrator had finally hit full blast as Zucchini Bellini still swung helplessly, unaware of the tragedy and loss below.

Adrenaline wouldn't let this cracker be deterred. Graham scrambled out over the sink and went carefully along the Dehydrator to Zucchini. His heart had cracked into a million pieces.

Detective Crackery would at least salvage one life tonight.

Graham saw another red-vine rope wrapped around the sink head near him. With tears and sink-water-stained eyes, he leaned over and stretched his hand out to grab it. The vine was just far enough away and much too slippery to stay in Graham's left hand.

He almost tossed his cookies knowing what he had to do next.

Placing out his palm with sheer will, Graham used Marsha's remaining stickiness to glob onto the vine and pull it closer.

Marsha was still helping him out, even after she fell to her melt.

Graham secured the vine and turned to face Zucchini, needing more slack.

"Zuch! Grab the vine!" shouted Graham over the roar of the sink.

The heir to the Bellini fortune swung limp in his trap, unflinching at the voice piercing the roar of the sink.

"Can you hear me?" Graham shouted again, squinting his eyes to make out a faint thumbs-up from Zucchini.

Breathing a sigh of relief, Graham almost smiled when he shouted, "When I toss it, you grab it!"

Graham successfully hooked the end on Zuch's foot on the first throw. Zucchini moved his other foot on top of the vine and held his feet together tightly. Graham tightened his grip and pulled the limp Zuch closer. They were finally out of the way of danger and away from the drop.

"W..what is that on your hand, Detective?" huffed an exhausted and painfully unaware Bellini.

Graham ignored the ignorant question and dove into work.

Crackery rapidly tied the red-vine rope around his feet while untying the other end of the from around Zuch's foot.

Graham then secured the end of the rope to the Sink head, turned to Zucchini with steadfastness and, gave instructions:

"I need your help! I need to go after her! When you feel the vine tug THREE times, pull me up. Two tugs mean give me more slack if you can. Got it?"

"Oh, my gourd..." before Zucchini could even process the situation, Graham dove into the Dehydrator after his love.

Soaring down through the heat, the daring detective rapidly approached the bottom, racing his sweat down to the bottom.

Without warning, the vine snapped hard around his ankles. They cracked slightly, but the heat helped to soften the crunch.

"OOOF" grunted the broken but still alive cracker.

He wiped away beads of sweat and squinted. Bursts of steam could be heard in every direction. The beast that was the Dehydrator was alive and hungry for more unwitting Food.

Graham began shouting for Marsha. His voice went hoarse quickly, but deep down, he knew she was no longer there.

"*Marsha! Marsha Mallow!*" *thinking somehow her last name amplified his urgency for her to hear.*

Knowing he couldn't stay much longer, Graham felt his body getting softer from the heat. The vine began cutting into his legs like a warm knife on a cool butter eve.

It was time to go. There was no more time for grief, he needed to make moves soon.

"I'll miss you," he whispered quietly through tears then added, "I'm sorry."

As Graham reached to tug the vine to have Zucchini pull him up, the last gift Graham had given Marsha, her bright pink headband appeared hooked on a stray metal rod below him. He reached for it with everything he had and a little of what she had left.

Millimeters before Graham could reach the fallen headband, he felt the rope tug him out of the Dehydrator, aggressively.

"NOOOOO!" echoed Graham's desperate cries. He watched her headband fade into the unusually cotton-candy-thick fog and disappear.

The detective had to be somewhat friendly to his important client once he was pulled to safety. But heir or no heir, Graham was in no mood to pretend. He decided he was going to let that green goon have it for pulling him up too early.

Among Graham's many racing thoughts as he ascended rapidly to the light, one stuck out to him, 'How is he able to pull me up so quickly? Zuch could hardly move when I left him. There's no way that half-wit suddenly grew muscles.'

The closer to the top Graham was getting, the more he could see the yellow and green of the CHEESE car lights bouncing off the interior walls of The Dehydrator.

Graham was quickly pulled free and clear of the massive steaming maw as it began shutting down. The Dehydrator needed to literally blow off tremendous blasts of steam from the pressure that had built up.

The blast spanned inside and out of the behemoth. One final explosion erupted from the top just as Graham was pulled out and rolled to safety; hat in hand, coattails slightly burnt.

Graham squared over onto his back and caught his breath just in time to have his questions about Zucchini's superfood strength answered. It wasn't the weak, green hands of Zucchini that pulled him up and out to safety, it was the crumbly, crackered-hands of Sylvester Moore.

Where relief should have been in a familiar face, instead was taken over by a wave of ever-growing anger. Graham tripped over the vines still tied around his feet trying to catch up to Sylvester.

"What are you doing here!?" yelled Graham, breathing heavily from confusion and exhaustion. The Sink had finally quieted down. The fuming detective had not.

"Where's Zucchini!?"

Sylvester, calmer than he should have been, took a lick of a candy cane and casually answered, "He's fine. He's having a cup of coco-coffee with the CHEESE officers."

Bewildered by Sylvester's reaction, Graham stood up and looked his orphan brother square in the face, holding back his remaining crack-up. That would be reserved for the unfortunate staff on call at the CHEESE station later that night.

"Did you send Marsha after me tonight?" Graham cracked his knuckles to show he wasn't playing anymore as he asked Sylvester with a shaky voice.

"I didn't SEND her." Sylvester turned to walk away. He stopped and turned only his head to look once more at Graham, "but I didn't tell her not to either. Later Cracker face."

Graham woke up swinging his fists. Parchment-paper sheets

everywhere, Coco and Artie, mid coco-coffee sip, were staring in concern.

12

Chapter Eleven: The Dehydrator Part Deux

"What? Haven't you ever had a recurring dream that shakes you out of sleep? Or is that just me?" Graham shook off the dream with a sip of an old, cold cup of coco-coffee and casually sat down as if nothing happened, "So, what were *you* talking about?"

The overall clues and facts of the case of the missing Peppercorn Pipe were being discussed by each of the three varying levels of detectives.

Concerns were addressed, theories were shared about the case, but ultimately, it all came down to Graham's return to the scene of the crime. The scene where both Sylvester and Marsha were last seen. The Dehydrator Part Deux.

"Artie. Cocoa." Graham looked at each of them with a sorrowful, tired face. He was leaning over as he spoke.

"I think that, from here on out, I'm going to close this case on my own."

The silence in the room became palpable. Cocoa wasn't about to argue with Graham, he understood Graham would have his reasons.

Artie leaned forward to speak, but Cocoa held her back, letting Graham continue.

"Artie, you did great today with the Mayor, but I'm going to need you to stick to taxi driving. I can't put you in any more danger." Artie hid her disappointment well and nodded in agreement.. She felt like Butter Sticarus, flying too close to the sun.

"Cocoa," Graham put his hand on Cocoa's shoulder.

"You're the best pal any Food could have. You've been stuck with me through a lot, but now it's time you start your candy cane shop and walk away from all of this."

Graham handed Cocoa a check.

"It's not much, but it's a new start for you. A much safer one."

Coco looked down at the check causing a single tear gumdrop to land on this life-changing paper.

All three of them stood up in unison. No words needed to be spoken at this juncture. They all knew where the detective had to go and what he had to revisit. Graham sat alone and in silence for a long time after the team departed.

All signs pointed to the Mayor's involvement. But Graham still couldn't prove it yet. Jordan's comment about Graham following after Marsha was the final clue; The detective would find the Pipe at the bottom of the Dehydrator.

"That's why my dreams have been so vivid lately." Graham thought out loud standing at the foot of the massive Dehydrator a few hours later. It somehow looked smaller and less menacing during the day.

The Detective bent down to sift his hands through the dried crumbs around the exit of The Dehydrator's bottom ventilator.

There were no tracks in or out of the emergency exit. Nothing around the door at all to suggest anything had been broken into. The only tracks that remained were the detectives.

It had been over a month, but the scene still hadn't been tampered with. CHEESE was unusually slow in this case and Graham didn't have the stomach to do the leg work for them this time.

There was so much litigation back and forth in the Cereal Courts. The crime scene just sat, thanks in part to the Gummy's involvement in delaying any movement. Who knew when the investigation would open back up? Especially now that Yellow Gummy Jr was gone and the feds were off the Gummy's back.

"Stop and think." Graham said to himself, once again licking another candied cane to concentrate.

Deep breath in.

Deep breath out.

Detective Crackery followed his sightline up the Dehydrator walls when something stopped him; there were red streaks slashed on the side of the machine.

"How had these gone unnoticed all this time?' Graham mumbled to himself.

"Only one thing could make this red..." guessed Graham.

"Ah ha!"

He looked down and noticed along a small section of the Dehydrator was an unusual growth sprouting out. Crackery picked up a cut piece of red vine. He wasn't sure if this was used to climb up on or down from the mechanical beast. Graham did know one thing; this was not the vine he was using that fateful night.This was placed here on purpose, and by the feel of it, recently.

Circling the massive, silo-like Dehydrator for the final time unable to see the top, Graham pushed through his fears and moved aside the CHEESE string tape that spiderwebbed across the exit doors to where maintenance could come and go from the Dehydrator. The massive doors slammed shut behind him, cutting his vision immediately.

Empty. Dark. Cold.

Graham carefully stepped around before tripping and almost falling over a small protrusion. He bent down to pick it up and realized it was Marsha's pink headband, or at least it looked like a headband. It was missing the signature double M initials stitched into the side.

The headband was being used as a wrap to hold what felt like a long, cylindrical item. Graham carefully unfurled the counterfeit cloth and felt a heavy thud in his palm.

The Peppercorn Pipe was preserved.

"Perfect," puffed a sigh of relief from Graham's held breath. He examined the headband again. Whoever put this here wanted Graham. The Pipe was the bait.

Quick pain in the back of the head.

Lights out.

Graham looked across the table at Marsha. They were enjoying their favorite table at their favorite restaurant, Le Legume Louie.

Marsha held Graham's hand lightly, not her usual warm grip. He could feel her slipping away in every sense.

She brushed her hair away from her eyes in a way that Graham adored. A careless brush away, as if she was walking through low-hanging broccoli trees. He handed her the gift he'd carefully wrapped.

"Happy Anniversary. This might help." offered Graham. In the past, his gift giving abilities had been spot on. They dwindled in

creative nature as time went on, as their lives went in different directions.

Detective work had made him weary. Unable to enjoy any form of vacation away from the hustle and bustle of Kitchentown.

However, Marsha's rise in her career and her work with Mabel opened up new doors on a daily basis.

Marsha was outgrowing more than just her small office; she was moving onto big things and one day she would run for Mayor. A place she could truly transform Kitchentown for the better.

Graham's bitterness and contempt grew daily for the Mayor and Marsha's partnership as the DA. It ultimately pushed him further from Marsha and created an unscalable wedge between them.

Marsha slowly opened the small box to reveal a neatly folded, crisp headband. Pink, Graham and Marsha's favorite color, and Marsha's initials stitched into the side.

Marsha had a habit of fidgeting her fingers when she was working out a problem, which made these stitched letters a helpful sensory tool.

DA Mallow's reaction was less than cool. She offered bland thank you followed by a gift of her own. Not one Graham wanted, but one he needed. She cleared her throat and put aside his gift.

"Graham, you know you're always going to have a special place in my gooey center. But I'm growing in my career and your support hasn't come with me." She hesitated a beat, took a breath and continued, "We should just chill things down for a bit. I hope you can understand."

Graham stopped eating. He somehow knew the end was inevitable. He just couldn't prepare himself quite yet.

At that moment, both Graham and Marsha's phones each began to buzz. A saving grace and a place to look other than the pain on each other's faces. Marsha reached first.

"It's Mabel, we're finishing up a case and she needs a quote."

Then, to the phone and ignoring Graham reaching for his phone.

"Hi, Mabel." Marsha's voice went quieter. "No better time than the present. What's going on?"

Marsha covered the receiver and mouthed to Graham. "I have to take this. We can talk later, if you want."

Graham took one last long look at his fading love. His eyes said more than he could muster.

Marsha shared the same look and went back to her call. "What's the address?"

Graham was placing his Cookie card back in his wallet while he answered his own Cracker Phone. "Detective Crackery, go ahead," answered Graham, trying to keep his voice all business.

"He's where?"

The rushed Detective stood up so fast his seat fell over. He hung up and apologized for the commotion to each of the onlookers.

"They found Zucchini Bellini, he's tied up above the Sink, I have to go." Graham lingered for one last beat seeing Marsha's sweet face for the last time as someone that wouldn't be a stranger to him.

"..Look at me. Don't disappoint, Detective, look up!" the same gruff voice from his dream shook Graham back to reality.

It was hard for Graham to look up when he wasn't aware which direction that actually was. Then, finally, the voice that shook him from his dream, crumbled on, "You and I both know you weren't getting to the Fridge on time."

Everything around the Detective was blurry, especially the very alive, large ball of yellow standing in front of him.

"I thought you were supposed to be dead?"

Yellow Gummy Jr lumbered up to the dazed and confused Detective, put a big yellow paw on Graham's red-vine tied up shoulder, and whispered with his sticky, slimy smile, "Sorry ta disappoint, detective."

13

Chapter Twelve: The Smoking Pipe

The smell of Yellow Gummy Jr's breath was enough to awaken any Food.

"You should probably freshen up that breath of yours," murmured Graham, more fully awake and more aware of his current situation. "I know it stinks down here, but that could partially be you."

In front of him loomed Yellow Gummy Jr in a dimly lit basement under the Fridge.

The Fridge floor was the part of town where the Gummy Family knew the CHEESE wouldn't venture. When The Dehydrator was shut down, they set up shop in the basement to dispose of unwanted Foods, kicked underneath to be forgotten about forever.

Graham's wrists began to crack from the tightened red vines that held him to the chair.

Jr. kept his composure over the detective's shoddy attempt to shake him up and grabbed a chair in front of him, keeping his strong breath aimed in Graham's face.

"Ya know, you're funny. Always kept my family laughing." The hulking bear stood up to grab a bucket in the corner filled to the brim with an unknown white liquid. "We'd laugh and laugh and *laugh*!" Yellow Gummy grunted out the last word as he tossed half of the bucket, drenching Graham.

'Milk,' thought Graham. It was never a good idea to soften up a Crackery unless they're being prepared for a rough time.

Graham carefully licked his softening lips and said through sloppy words, "Ya know, with milk; I'm not half bad. But, tell me something. Speaking of bad, how are you still alive?"

"Thanks to your girlfriend, may she rest in pieces, there weren just too many investigations piling up on my family. Ya see, us Gummy's tend to specialize in the expiration business."

Yellow Gummy Jr decided to painfully bearsplain the obvious to Graham.

Yellow winked and continued. "It's awfully tough to investigate a grieving family."

"It was odd seeing your picture on Tea-V that day. You look much worse in real life. Especially for expired Food." Graham spit as he finished his sentence.

Yellow Gummy Jr sat down annoyed with Graham's reluctance to give in, but with the next revelation, Yellow may have gotten his way.

"Your brother Sylvester, my old pal, didn't talk this much when he was in your seat. But, then again, he's much quieter these days."

Graham couldn't hide his emotion, but he knew he couldn't react with too much physical strength. He would tear in two pieces easily in his sopping state.

Besides, this Gummy was smarter than the average bear, he'd made it impossible to lose a physical battle with a superior detective.

"Well, Sylvester was always drawn to rotten Food," Graham said through gritted teeth. He could feel his body drying and his strength returning. But there was always the second half of that bucket for Yellow's backup if Graham kept cracking wise.

"Where is he now?" Graham asked, unable to mask his fear.

Yellow walked over to a table and picked up the Peppercorn Pipe. Then, he walked back over to Graham, marveling at the Pipe the whole time. Stalling to make a nervous Crackery more anxious.

"Sylvester always had high hopes, ya know?" Junior began his story. He wasn't one to waste words. He would pontificate, but there was always a point to the alphabet soup of nonsense that he spewed.

"Sly was always so angry; jealous, actually. He saw your friendships blossom and business grow while he sat stunted in a garden of failure."

Gummy continued examining the Pipe, while he spoke.

"Business after business took a couple of pieces from Sylvester: his energy and his money. What did it give back in return? Debts. Loss. Frustration." Yellow pointed to each finger with the Pipe as he listed Sylvester's problems.

Graham's patience was being tested, and so were the red vine ropes starting to loosen as Graham began to take his shape once again.

"Yessir, the tale of two Crackery's." Yellow stood up again and walked away, back turned to Graham.

"One got chewed up and spit out of Kitchentown," Yellow turned his head to wink at Graham, "That's you."

He walked over to switch on a light in the corner.

"The other, well, like I said; he had high apple pie in the sky hopes."

Yellow walked over to a large basin with a tarp covering the top from view. He lifted the cover and tossed it aside to reveal it was fully packed down with a patchy graham cracker crust.

Graham felt like he was going to be sick. Not only at the horrible ending Sylvester faced, but the knowledge that he'd be filling in the patches.

Yellow Gummy Jr patted Graham on the back.

"Don't be too hard on yourself. You two are a lot alike. Both losers, both abandoned at birth." Yellow took a step and motioned for the bucket.

"And he had the same look on his face as you do now. In the same chair too! Isn't that something? It's a good thing he told us all about you before we, well." Yellow smiled, "Before he *packed up* and left for good."

Graham flinched but kept his cool and fired back, "If you think Sylvester was a loser, why do you believe all the things he told you about me." Graham mocked. "Seems like you're the sucker."

One of the many things Detective Crackery had learned over many tussles with the Gummy's is their impatience. Yellow Gummy Jr grew visibly guttural and growling in his speech. Less Gummy, more bear. He started rambling, growling out his list:

"Point is, I already have several buyers lined up to pay One Fortune Cookie, or Three Fortune Cookies, even up to Fifteen Fortune Cookies!" Yellow let out a booming roar that was also half laugh. "You're not chewing this one up for me!"

Junior rose to his full height, looming over Graham.

"My family wants you to crumble. Swept up, and tossed out with the trash where you belong. You're stale, and now your time has expired!

"For too long, you've been the jalapeno burning my family's eyes. Constantly being the thorn in our paws. Now," Yellow took a few steps off to Graham's side, just out of sight, "you'll be joining ol' Sly here to finish off the crust."

Yellow leaned down and picked up a vanilla folder on a table just out of sight.

"Don't worry, you two boys can make amends. We'll be bringing you Mabel's sticky company as well to top off this pie!" Junior tossed several cut-out articles from the Kitchentown Crier of the Gummy's alleged crimes, all written by Mabel Seerup, aided by the District Attorney, Marsha Mallow.

"So, you used Sylvester to get into my world and rip it apart. Now, you're destroying anyone getting in your way, even after you get rid of me?" Graham piecing it all together as he reiterated it to Yellow.

After all, Detective Crackery needed a wall on which to bounce his thoughts.

The confounded Gummy stood still, listening. Usually, he was the one rattling off the plans to his victims, not the other way around.

"You offed Marsha because she was getting too close to exposing some of your family's crimes and you figured you might as well pay to keep the Mayor in your pocket anyway after Marsha was gone." Graham continued listing the Gummy's crimes.

"You off me next." Graham cleared his throat, mentioning himself.

"Then you're going to get rid of Mabel because she decided to keep your rotten family accountable for your crimes." Graham finished listing each Food the Gummy's wanted to dispose of as if he was reading a checklist from the Good Cook Book.

Yellow began uncomfortably shifting in his chair as Graham continued.

"What I can't figure out is why Mike? You probably could have split the profits from the Pipe with him."

It all clicked for Detective Crackery at that moment.

"So, *that's* why you changed your name and the Alltaste insurance policy to something as stupid as, 'Sal Minelli'?" Graham asked mockingly.

Yellow smiled and rose slowly as Graham rounded the end. "Or is Sal the alter ego of your mold in the CHEESE station," Graham tested out how that information would strike the bear, maybe he'd admit Bleu had done Kitchentown dirty after all.

At the disappointment of Graham, Yellow didn't react, which

forced the detective to continue.

"You can 86 me, but just know, there will always be others to help take you down." Graham stalled, almost free from his binds.

"Others you don't even know about." Crackery leaned back in his chair to give his wrists more slack and finally free his hands.

No sooner did Graham's wrists become free of the red vines when the remaining bucket of milk descended on Graham's back like a tidal wave of doom from an unseen assailant.

Graham was immediately sopping wet from head to toe. Any sudden moves could permanently disfigure him if he dried that way.

If he would have time to dry at all.

One eye was immediately washed shut, unable to open again.

The other had milk dripping down, obstructing most of his view, but still, Graham was able to spot another figure in the room.

"I must be hallucinating, Yellow. You're large, but now I'm seeing double." Even dripping wet, Graham kept his wits about him.

When he finally noticed the other yellow figure looming next to Yellow Gummy Jr, he realized he wasn't seeing double. He was in big trouble.

"Mike?" he whispered.

"Is that all you can muster?" sneered the grossly familiar face of Mike Mustardereli.

"It's Sal, by the way, Sal Minelli. I see you got my messages, eh buddy?" Mike A.K.A. Sal, tossed several copies of his threatening magnet-letter to Graham.

"You two waste a lot of paper, you know that?" Graham hid his shock from his resurrected friend.

"So, which one of you two lovely fella's impersonated Marsha for my answering machine? Looks like Sylvester *did* give you some accurate info after all." Crackery was careful to move sparingly.

Sal jumped up and down with his hand raised in the air with mocking excitement, "Ooh! Ooh! That was me!" snickering at his own explanation.

"Mabel and Marsha tended to record some of their calls in case something ever happened to either of them. They needed proof of what they worked on."

Sal pulled out a recorder and played Marsha humming her favorite song, Old Cookie Moon, from one of the recordings where she was waiting for Mabel to join the call. She sounded just as Graham heard on his answering machine a few days ago.

"Stealing a recorder and then getting rid of your girlfriend? Real classy move. What makes you think you'll outsmart her?" taunted Graham.

Sal cackled, "No, detective, my sticky bun had a lot of dirt on some important people that employ me. The recorder was more of a souvenir than a theft."

Sal grew more serious now. His voice was low and booming off the walls of the Fridge Basement. A baritone Graham didn't know existed in his previously anxious and chipper friend.

"She won't be needing it too much longer anyway."

Whether it was the drying milk on Graham's disfigured frame, the loss he continuously suffered, the revelation that the dead could come back at any moment, coupled with Bleu's back being turned on the law – it all made the hollowed detective feel empty.

He wasn't cracking up. He was cracking apart.

Sal continued while tossing the recorder at Graham's slump-ing body.

"You don't think your pal Mr. Lattely wants a successful candy cane shop? Or that your little stalk friend wants to follow in your footsteps? Let alone walk at all?" threatened the true form of Sal Minelli. Graham couldn't stomach these horrible words coming out of a once friendly face.

"This ain't my first rodeo being expired and getting a fresh start. But thanks to you, Mabel and Marsha, it's getting exhausting starting over." Sal sat down hard on a nearby chair now sitting face to face with Graham.

"That's who you are." Graham exclaimed with a sense of relief.

"You're just another rotten Food that got tangled up with the Gummy's. You're nobody." The word 'nobody' echoed off the walls.

Graham continued with his insults.

"Just like your dopey bear friend over here. You're both just mediocre, lukewarm nothings." Crackery let the word land hoping to buy any amount of time.

Both yellow hulking figures rose aggressively. Each grabbed the detective by the shoulders, squeezing harder to disfigure him more and crack him where he was dry.

Graham was being hauled to his final destination, the Pie Cruster. He noticed it was still not rinsed off from Sylvester's previous turn.

Graham was tossed abruptly below the ominous large, metallic circle of the Cruster. Yellow Gummy Jr moved towards the switch that turned on the machine.

Sal leaned in close to Crackery's battered frame, "Any last words, detective?"

Crackery noticed the faint sight of CHEESE lights in the background as he fought consciousness.

The milk had done significant damage and the Cruster was about to clean his plate for good.

Graham's open eye closed slowly as he whispered out one final message to his captors before fading to black.

"I'll...see you...in jell...o."

For the first time since Marsha passed, Graham awoke, not from a nightmare or horrific memory, but instead feeling peace. Getting to the bottom of this case helped him find his purpose once again.

The room was filled with chirping machines spelling out the detective's regaining vitals. "Where am I?" whispered Graham to a seemingly empty room.

His only viewpoint was aimed up at the ceiling at an angle. Out of his periphery, up popped a green, pointed mop top.

"Hiya Detective! You're back!" Artie hopped up and down to let Graham know she was with him.

Another familiar voice came into the room.

"He's awake?" Cocoa's hat sailed across the room before he entered, landing impossibly softly on top of Graham's bandaged head.

Graham smiled at his two closest friends and confidants before seizing up in fear. He knew the two most sinister creeps in Kitchentown had him in a sticky situation what felt like minutes ago. "Wait, where are they?"

Graham was unable to move, he was still in painful recovery. Cocoa put a hand on Graham's shoulder and calmed his friend.

"You're fine, they're far away now. All is safe. Artie, here..."

Artie excitedly interrupted Cocoa's retelling.

"I was tracking you and brought the CHEESE to the Fridge

Floor!"

Artie could read confusion, rather than gratefulness on the detective's face. She then explained much slower and in more detail.

"When we left the Hellman Building, I had Cocoa give me access to view your Cracker Tracker on your phone, ya know – in case." shrugged Artie.

After a brief moment of annoyance, Graham's eyes softened from frustrated to grateful.

"I know, it was wrong not to tell you and I'm sorry. But you're alive, right?" smiled Cocoa, putting his arm around Artie in appreciation.

Crackery was in pain and unable to move until his procedure of reshaping was complete. Cocoa gathered Artie and as they left, he placed a copy of the Kitchentown Crier open in Graham's view.

"We'll talk more tomorrow about what happened. You need a break. In the meantime, have a read and get some rest." Cocoa winked, and along with Artie, faded from view.

Graham smiled as they walked away. His smile grew wider looking down now at the article below. Written by the very much alive, Mabel Seerup. All he could see besides her name was the title.

Detective Crackery is Back! So is the Peppercorn Pipe.

The piece talked very complimentary about Graham's return to the detective world and how the return of the Peppercorn Pipe would be a defining moment in an already all-star career.

While the acclaim and recognition for a job well done was nice to read, Graham was more focused on finding out the fate of his captors.

Graham whispered out loud as he read from the article.

"The CHEESE didn't stand alone this time. Detective Crackery's cohorts, Cocoa Lattely and Artie Chokerode informed Lieutenant Gouda early this morning of Graham's disappearance and subsequent location. Thanks in part to his Cracker Tracker app on his phone."

He stopped reading to wipe a gumdrop tear from his eye. He wasn't fully realizing how his life was spared and the impact it was having on him.

Sniffing, Graham continued to read further.

"The CHEESE were called to the Fridge Floor where a very much alive Yellow Gummy Jr and Salvatore Minielli A.K.A. Mike Mustardereli, was preparing to crush Detective Crackery into Pie Crust. Finding Detective Crackery also helped the CHEESE discover the whereabouts of Sylvester Moore, another captive and casualty of the Gummy crime family.

Sources indicate Sal Minelli, blubbering, immediately surrendered to the CHEESE while Yellow Gummy Jr fought the law, but the law won, thanks to the help and quick thinking of Lieutenant Gouda. Woah!'' Graham interrupted his reading and was stunned. Someone he treated so poorly in the past saved his life.

Exhaustion was starting to crepe over Graham like a warm blanket. He knew he needed rest, but also wanted to finish the Crier's account of what happened. The detective wearily looked down and laughed as he read.

"Continued on page D2."

Graham pushed the paper away. He didn't have enough energy to turn the page. Crackery was asleep before the paper landed softly next to him on the floor.

14

Chapter Thirteen: Recovery

The next few days in the Hospital were rough for Graham. Tri-daily frosting baths which helped loosen him up, making it easier to put his correct shape back together again.

Crackery was in constant need of pain medications. A silver-lining amongst the turmoil was the various well-wishing Foods that stopped by here and there.

Detective Crackery was once again a welcome face in Kitchen-town, though it cost him more than most could know.

Penny and Petey Pickle even stopped by to deliver a hand-drawn message of hope that wished Graham would get well soon.

A few other guests trickled in, some unexpected.

"It sure does stink in here." Came the familiar and now friendly voice of Captain Gouda.

Graham reacted with a faint smile, realizing a sour friendship could be still ripened.

"It does now that you're here."

Gouda, now in street clothes, sat down next to Graham's

bedside. Graham was looking more like himself every day, but one eye was still drooping and didn't work as well as the other.

"It appears, we have a fence or two to mend," Graham commented to Gouda, who nodded in agreement.

"It's not your fault what happened to Marsha, and it's entirely my fault that, well." Graham looked down, embarrassed, "that you needed that bandage on your head for so long."

Gouda smiled and put his hand reassuringly on Graham's bedside.

"Let's let bite-gones be bite-gones. The important thing is you're recovering, and alive. Which is more than I can say for our Gummy friend," smiled Gouda, hoping to change the subject.

Fences were mended. Friends were born.

Graham finally noticed Gouda's arm in a sling.

"What happened there? Battle wounds?"

Gouda ignored the detective's question and pressed on.

"I'm fine. Occupational hazard."

Artie, who practically lived in Graham's room, could hardly contain herself when she heard this modest passive answer.

"Don't believe him, detective. He's a hero! Tell him, Captain!" Artie looked up admiringly at Gouda who simply smiled and shook his head slightly.

"Fine, then I will," Artie continued excitedly.

"After we gave your tracker information to the CHEESE, Cocoa and I raced over in a squad car immediately with a few officers."

Gouda stood up and walked toward the window to look out while his account was recounted.

"When we got there, you were in terrible shape. Oops," Artie realized his faux pas. Graham smiled at the turnip of phrase. Artie smiled back and continued.

"Anway, Gouda ran in, Cocoa and I followed behind and stayed at a *safe* distance," Artie looked at Gouda at the word 'safe' to show she was able to heed the Captain's words. She continued her story, excitedly. Gouda nodded back.

"The speed and veracity with which Gouda knocked Yellow Gummy Jr off of his paws was incredible!" Artie jumped up.

Graham jumped in to ask, "The paper said Mike, I mean Sal, gave up pretty quickly?"

Artie smiled, "Let's just say he was yellow in every way!"

Gouda walked back over to regain the room's composure.

"That was true," he stated matter-of-factly, then smiled and added, "and kind of funny."

Gouda, in a serious tone again, took a deep breath.

The Captain began reliving his encounter. He could still feel the fear from the sheer size of Yellow Gummy Jr's hulking presence.

Gouda remembered getting one solid shot of his peas shooter to hit Yellow Gummy Jr. Sadly, all it did was poke the bear which sent him into the darkness of the room. Gouda's heart began beating loudly at the thought.

"Tell him what you did next!" Artie excitedly said and then looked over at Graham, "It was insane!"

Gouda didn't have the heart to dive fully into detail. How could he? There was no time to process what had happened yet, let alone make it sound exciting.

Captain Gouda didn't want to share with the room the terror he felt for not being able to see in a dimly lit room that reeked of danger.

Graham didn't need to know the state of how badly he had been misshapen and how it turned Gouda's stomach to see.

The Captain of CHEESE didn't know how to describe the pouring sweat running down him as he tried to free Graham from this certain death trap. And he certainly didn't want to admit he was also terrified to permanently rearrange the drenched detective beyond repair. The potential guilt he would feel for failing was overwhelming.

Gouda remembered the deafening silence once he'd finally freed Graham and moved him to relative safety. It felt like the calm before the storm of Yellow Gummy Jr, now in full bear mode. Growling and standing to an intimidating height on his hind legs, bellowing in a blind rage.

Gouda didn't want to admit that his strength and cunning agility that allowed him to maneuver out of the way of a charging bear and then slam the Gummy into the Pie Cruster wasn't what actually occurred.

The appearance of the terrorizing bear sent Gouda stumbling backward, causing Junior to trip over the CHEESE officer's legs and fall into the Cruster just as the metal lid closed on him.

The recovering detective didn't need to know about the entrails that spouted out of the sides of the Cruster like a yellow tidal wave of goo. Nor did he need to know how it came down with unrelenting force and had to be carefully removed from the detective's healing body.

Captain Gouda looked across the aisle of Food before him: Artie, Graham, and a few candy-striper nurses pretending to work in the background, but secretly waiting to hear the Captain's response.

After all he'd been through, Gouda simply quoted Mabel's article dryly and said, "He fought the law, and the law won. Thanks to you two," Gouda looked down at Artie and up at the new arrival in the room, Cocoa. "The case is now closed and the Pipe is safely back where it belongs; in the CHEESE station for now." Gouda folded his arms and nodded, putting a period on the story.

"Thank you again, Captain, for your bravery." Cocoa gratefully shook the officer's hands and added, "You're a good CHEESE." He then turned to address Artie.

"Would you both mind giving Graham and I the room for a few minutes?"

Cocoa shut the door and turned just in time to take Graham's flying hat to the face.

"I always did have a terrible aim," chuckled Graham, feeling the spirits of those around him lift him higher than he'd felt in a long time.

Cocoa bent down slowly to pick up the hat. Graham could feel some bad news coming his way.

"What's wrong, bud?"

Cocoa sat down, unable to fully look at Graham, but pressed on.

"It's just seeing you mushed up like this...like you still are now." Cocoa looked up at Graham fully for the first time, fighting back his emotion.

"It's hard to watch you go through this. Not every case was bad, but this one..." Cocoa tailed off before continuing.

"We've been partners for a long time and even though I'm moving into the candied canes game you're still going to be a detective. And bad things will still happen to you." Cocoa motioned towards the Hospital equipment all around them. "It freaks me out a little bit. I feel like I'm leaving you at a bad time." Cocoa wiped away one big gumdrop tear.

The two friends sat quietly. Graham put a comforting hand on Cocoa's shoulder.

"I'm trying to get some *real* help to not get in these situations anymore," Graham smiled joking to lower the temperature in the room.

"You definitely need someone's help though, just not mine," Cocoa wiped his eyes and chuckled.

"I have just the Food for the occasion," Graham smiled.

15

Chapter Fourteen: Giveth and Baketh Away

The fourth morning in the Hospital was the final one for the soon-to-be-fully-healed detective. He'd regained most of his shape, though he still needed to walk with support. He was given a large, novelty Cane from a store coming soon: Cocoa's Cane's.

Graham and Artie were packing the detective's things up to leave and making sure all were accounted for when there was a knock at the door. They turned to see the warm smile and welcome face of Mabel Seerup.

Graham looked relieved, Artie was utterly speechless. She was too intimidated to say anything, so she sat quietly pretending to read the paper while keeping her eyes on Mabel during the entire visit.

"I didn't think you'd come," Graham joked and turned back to his bag.

"I always follow up with my sources. How are you getting around?" Mabel asked, walking in with her bag in hand and placing it next to the chair as she sat down. She gave a quick wave to Artie who nodded slightly before going back to the paper.

"Recovering, thanks to several well wishers, one CHEESEhead, and an article writer I happen to know."

Graham held up the copy of her article after the Pipe had been returned, holding onto it for his future self to remember.

"Thanks," Mabel said, then asked, "I suppose you didn't continue onto D2, huh?" she smiled.

Graham was astonished, "How did you know?"

"Read it later," retorted Mabel, "I'd know if you had read it. Trust me."

She smiled and continued.

"So, what's next for you, detective? Yellow Gummy Jr is out and my phony ex is where he belongs again, in the Jammer. Case closed?"

"Not quite yet." Graham reached into his bag and pulled out the recorder Gouda recovered from the scene. He held it in Mabel's direction without looking.

"There are a few more things to wrap up but I believe this belongs to you."

Mabel was surprised to see her recorder once again.

"Did you listen to any of it? It's everything Marsha and I had worked on for months."

"No," Graham reported. He looked over at Mabel. "It's kind of painful to hear Marsha's voice. Her and I were breaking up before she..." Graham hesitated and continued, "I'm just having trouble shaking that."

Mabel pushed the recorder back, keeping it in the detective's bruised hand.

"Give the last two recordings a listen. You can bring the recorder back anytime. Let's catchup when you're feeling better. Take care, Graham."

Mabel stood up to leave, when Artie finally summoned the courage to express her appreciation for her favorite writer, "You're great!" was all that squeaked out.

Artie wasn't accustomed to being nervous around famous Food, but this was different. Mabel smiled before Artie regained her composure and tried again, "Your articles have helped so much Food and I was hoping you'd be able to help me find my missing dad, too."

Mabel took out her pen and pad and quickly jotted down a few notes. When she capped her pen, instead of putting it back in her bag, Mabel smiled, handed it down to Artie, and said,

"I'll work with a good friend of mine to bring him back. Thanks for reading."

Mabel gave a quick wink to Graham and slipped out of the doorway leaving a confused Crackery staring at the recorder in his hand. Artie was feeling hopeful and excited at this new ally.

From the hallway they heard Mabel call out one last announce-ment:

"Please, continue on D2!"

Artie's Taxi pulled up and Graham hobbled into the backseat carrying his bag in tow.

"Home, Detective?" chirped Artie, already throwing the taxi into gear.

"I need to stop at my office first." Graham said while pulling out his folded up copy of the Kitchentown Crier along with the recorder and headphones.

Graham plugged in his headphones to the recorder and re-wound to the final recording between Marsha and Mabel:

Mabel Seerup's voice crackled over the low hum of the white

noise.

"So, are there any additional comments from the DAs office, I'm going to run the story tomorrow."

Marsha's voice was up next.

"No comment. Not until the Mayor has his say first, I'm not trying to overstep my bounds."

There was a beat before Marsha continued, sounding more excited and eager this time.

"I just need to overstep these bounds at some point. There has to be more we can do in Kitchentown than these constraints allow."

Mabel's voice chimed back in.

"Then let's stop talking about it, and finally launch our own Peas in a Podcast: 'Kitchentown Crimes.' We can really get into facts and not play it safe through all of this red bubble tape. We can do it our way."

Marsha was silent for a few moments, then quietly said, *"You know what, let's do this. I'm tired of asking, it's time to start telling."*

At that moment, the sound of a door bursting open crashed the excitement of new possibilities. Jordan's out-of-breath voice huffed onto the recording.

"Hi, I'm so sorry I'm late, Bobbi and I were just. Well, I'm here."

The awkward silence was palpable at this odd admission. Something Graham felt instant relief over. He'd always had a jealous eye towards the Mayor, but that seemed unnecessary now.

Mabel's voice cut the tension.

"Sir, I was asking Marsha if there were any comments from the Hellman Building before I file this article regarding the Gummy's latest kidnapping attempt."

Jordan, catching his breath by taking one large one, sighed.

"I say we go with whatever Marsha thinks. Gourd knows the

Gummy's are going to kidnap anyone they can for a buck. I've heard that dopey Bellini kid is next. Wouldn't that be rich?" The Mayor's scoff reverberated in Graham's headphones.

The tape fizzed out after the laugh, paving the way for a few moments of silence before crackling back in again.

This time, the recording was just between Mabel and Mayor Naise. A sadness lingered in the air over and throughout their conversation.

"How are you holding up?"

They both asked each other simultaneously.

Mabel talked first.

"It's never easy to lose a best friend. Then find out your ex is a criminal in the Gummy gang and then get threats from that same gang. But, how are YOU doing?" Asked Mabel sarcastically.

"Awful." Came the quiet, mournful voice of the Mayor. A tone he had never projected to the public before.

"Marsha changed things in this town for the good, and forever," he sniffed.

"She will be missed dearly. Bobbi and I are going to the memorial together this week, what about you?" He blew his nose loudly before Mabel could respond.

"I don't know," She hesitated and continued. *"I can't look at Graham. He's been through so much and we still have to lie to him about what's really going on with Mike, I mean Sal."* She huffed out of frustration at her recent revelation.

The Mayor stepped in, *"It's for his own benefit. Besides, we still need to sort out how to handle Bleu as the mold in the CHEESE department. He was like the father Graham never had."*

Marsha clearly had shared this information with the Mayor. Graham didn't realize how much people around him were actually invested in his work and cared about him as a Food. Jordan's voice continued as Graham listened with a new understanding. *"Until then, we can try and figure out if Yellow Gummy Jr is actually gone or simply, "expired."*

Jordan emphasized that last phrase.

Mabel pressed on, asking her usual final question.

"Any comment from the Hellman Building?"

The Mayor hesitated, taking a deep breath.

"Off, off, off the record?"

"Sure"

Another deep breath from the Mayor.

"Bobbi and I were discussing this last night: Graham already sees me as a corrupt politician so I should just lean into it until the truth comes out and see if Graham still forgives me. Hopefully, he'll start to trust me going forward."

Mabel simply huffed in frustration, but Jordan's voice continued over the recording.

"Bobbi already sent Bleu the samples from my office, for the unknowing detective. So we're committed now. Might as well use the mold to our advantage before removing it from CHEESE."

"So, no comment then?"

Mabel asked one more time. Then a long period of silence until Mayor Naise quietly said,

"No comment."

As the recording fizzled out, Graham removed his headphones. He felt the weight of his fears lift off with them. The recording helped Graham feel hope and peace for the first time, perhaps in his life.

Through this tragedy, Detective Crackery was given a few more surprising pieces of his own puzzle to complete:

The Mayor wasn't a total monster. Gouda wasn't a bad CHEESE officer, Bleu was. Marsha and Mabel were doing the most with the least and not getting a lot of credit for it. Especially from Graham himself.

Even though his one eye was still wrapped in a bandage, it was clear to Graham, he could see that *he* was ultimately what drove Marsha and him apart. Not their careers, but instead his jealousy and immaturity.

"Why do you have an old paper with you?" Artie asked, peering into the rearview mirror at the bandaged detective.

"Hoarding it because your name is back?" chuckled Artie.

Graham smiled, "I promised someone I'd finish their story." he said, continuing to D2.

It was the full account from Cocoa's perspective. He described what Gouda did to save Graham, in full detail. The article described each part:

From Graham's harrowing rescue to Yellow Gummy Jr going full bear and stalking Gouda in the darkened room.

He read that after Gouda ended Yellow in the Pie Cruster, Gouda tried to protect Graham from the outpouring of Gummy goo, but was unsuccessful.

Graham continued to read about how Sal Minelli is back in a maximum cookie prison. Expiration would be impossible this time. Bleu had been named, arrested, and ousted from CHEESE as the mold. Graham was still devastated by his mentor's decision to turn on the very town he'd vow to keep safe.

The Gummy's bought Bleu for a decent retirement since the aging CHEESE Captain had spent his life never saving. Graham decided moving forward that he'd be a lot more careful who is welcome into his life.

The final two sections of the article held the detective's attention the strongest:

The first was a lengthy statement from the Mayor thanking

Graham for deftly bringing the Peppercorn Pipe back to its former glory and how Kitchentown owes him several debts of gratitude.

This was then followed by an open invitation for Graham to come to the Hellman Building. More than enough for Graham to work with Jordan moving forward.

Crackery lost Bleu but gained Naise.

The last paragraph held Graham's attention as the taxi pulled up to his office, waiting for his next move:

"This will be my last contribution to the Kitchentown Crier." Mabel wrote.

Graham was shocked.

"While I've loved almost every minute, and certainly helped make this city a little better; it's time I moved on."

As Mabel tended to do, she kept her goodbyes and thank yous short and sweet, leaving a mystery as to her next steps, but promised the readers they haven't heard the last from Mabel Seerup.

Graham folded up the paper with hidden astonishment, stuffed it back in his bag and looked up at Artie.

"Could you drive around the tile block for a little bit and come back shortly? I have a quick meeting."

Artie smiled and nodded.

"See you soon, Detective!"

She sped off before Graham could close the door.

Detective Crackery hobbled over and slowly unlocked the door to his office. It had been cleaned and was now teeming with various gift baskets, plants, and other assorted Get-Well-Soons.

Placed front and center on his desk was the biggest basket yet, from Cocoa's Canes.

Graham reached for the note with a smile, when his desk chair spun and a darkened figure smiled.

"Thank you for meeting me here." Graham announced calmly.

"It's no problem at all. Looks like you're feeling better." Muttered the voice. "So, what can I do for you, detective?" asked Mayor Naise.

16

Chapter Fifteen: Onward and Upward

The taxi sped along the early morning roads in Kitchentown. Graham, almost fully healed by now, was in the backseat pouring over fresh caseloads that had poured in over the last few weeks.

The air was certainly getting crisper near the Fridge. It was the time of year the Big Window started to close thanks to the gift of colder weather.

The taxi pulled up in front of Cocoa's Cane shop, the former home of Mike's Rare Monuments and Other Strings. Graham stepped out of the vehicle and buttoned up Sylvesters vest.

After the vest had been scrubbed of any devices by Captain Gouda, Graham had decided to implement it in his wardrobe as a badge of honor: To remember his lost brother but also a reminder of stinging betrayal.

Graham also kept the pink headband that held the Peppercorn Pipe. Gouda recovered it at the scene and Graham added the stitched M's for effect. He kept it in the breast pocket of the vest, close to his heart.

The new partnerships Graham developed would be there as a

support system unlike one the detective had seen before.

The bell to Cocoa's store jingled a welcoming noise to Graham who was popping in for his daily cane pick-up. As the door opened, both Graham's hat and Cocoa's passed each other mid-air to land perfectly on each other's smiling heads.

"How do you like the new digs?" Cocoa held out his arms to encompass the room.

"It's perfect. It's so you!" Graham exclaimed, popping a cane in his mouth excitedly looking around the room at the decor.

Displays of a multitude of canes lined the walls with the description of each flavor and intent written below it, all written with a comical, tongue-in-cheek humor.

The Tea-V was on in the background on mute when Jordan appeared on screen.

"Isn't this the press conference where you're supposed to be the star?" Cocoa said as he laughed and cranked the volume for all in the store to hear.

"Thank you everyone, thank you." The Mayor waved to the lukewarm crowd reaction.

"I want to start out with some unfortunate news. For some time now, there has been a mold in the CHEESE station," Jordan paused his speech for gasps in the audience at this betrayal.

"We have apprehended Roquefort M Bleu, the former CHEESE of Police. Efforts from multiple fronts led to the discovery that Bleu was working with the Gummy's to issue fake expiration dates for low-offending Foods. This in turn helped to send the 'leftovers' back on the streets to open up new avenues for the Gummy's to launder their stolen money."

The Mayor shuffled his notes and continued on. He wanted to shift the focus away from this horrific tragedy and into a more hopeful territory. "I've enacted a law that calls to hire a baker's dozens of CHEESE officers and investigators to find all Expired Foods still at large. We will pull their phony licenses, send them back to the Jammer, and offer those locations up to legitimate Food business owners in the area."

Graham and Cocoa high-fived without even looking over at each other.

"Kitchentown owes a tremendous thank you to the new and courageous Captain of CHEESE, Hall N Gouda. Your bravery... " The mayor was immediately interrupted by a thunderous applause.

Jordan continued speaking over the roar of applause and cheers, "Your bravery helped rid Kitchentown of the Yellow Gummy Jr scourge."

Thunderous applause exploded again, almost knocking the Mayor over as the camera panned over to Gouda, who sat and waved in simple acknowledgement. Jordan continued his list of thank you's.:

"Thanks also to Artie Chokerode and Cocoa Lattely for their help in finding, and ultimately saving, Detective Crackery by alerting the authorities quickly. Without them, we would have lost this city's best detective."

Graham turned to see Artie celebrating the news conference he was listening to in the waiting taxi and smiled.

The Mayor continued riding the applause with further announcements.

"Thanks to that discovery, The Gummy family, while having disappeared into hiding once again, is now officially under continued investigation. The charges are for their role in the kidnapping of Zucchini Bellini, shoddy construction work on the Dehydrator, and ultimately, the death of Marsha Mallow, Kitchentown's finest District Attorney."

After respectful applause from the audience, the mayor led everyone in a moment of silence for their fallen fellow Food. A time of reflection for all about what it meant to lose someone important in Kitchentown.

After a moment, the Mayor looked up, cleared his throat, and continued.

"Finally, we thank the courage, dedication, and intelligence of Detective Crackery. He was able to solve the case and return our precious Peppercorn Pipe to its rightful place. It will now sit, well guarded, inside the Hellman Building." The roar of applause continued on for sometime, the camera panning, searching for a detective that wouldn't be found.

"Don't you want to take a bow?" joked Cocoa, turning down the Tea-V and looking up in time to see Graham walking out of the door. He was never one for the limelight.

Epilogue

From the moment Graham decided to become a detective until the case of the Missing Peppercorn Pipe was closed, he imagined what his life would be like:

Solving low-level crimes, embracing a quiet life amongst the Food in Kitchentown. Maybe settling down with Marsha and having a few crackerlings and malloweens of their own.

Graham's life, however, was far from ordinary. He was more impulsive. Meticulous plans were never his specialty.

After he lost Marsha, Crackery was a cracked and broken detective, down on his luck and feeling hopelessly alone.

But, like all of us, being torn down can toughen us up and help us become more whole in the end.

Detective Crackery decided it was finally time to shake the crust off of his bread shoes and get his life back in some working order.

Captain Gouda rose above Roquefort Bleu. Cocoa cut out on his own to run his Cane shop, but Artie was the perfect filling for Graham as his new, Junior detective.

As for me, my article writing days are over. Traded in for the Peas in the Podcast Production. With the pension offered from Kitchentown and my new-found life, I'd like to welcome all my first time listeners to the first episode of Mabel Seerup presents the Adventures of Graham Crackery, Food Detective.

The End

About the Author

Peter prefers puns to soliloquies and almost always avoids alliteration. As a former copywriter and more recent recruiter for Wawa, Peter's dream of launching a debut novel, filled to the brim with ridiculousness, has finally come true. An avid eater of foods and cooker of decent meals, Peter combined his love of humor, food, and storytelling to bring Graham and his Food friends to life. Peter also wanted to take the time to thank everyone that read his story and even those that have gotten this far into the About the Author page. So, Thanks!

You can connect with me on:
🌐 http://grahamcrackery.com